THE GUY NEXT DOOR

Toni Blake

Dear Reader,

This is one of three books published at the beginning of my career under the pen name Toni Blair. Unfortunately, when they first released in the late 90s, the length limitations of the publisher required these novels to be shortened by approximately one-third of their original length, altering my vision for the stories significantly. So I'm pleased to be able to present, for the first time anywhere, the full and extended versions of these books.

As I read over my original manuscripts and polished up the words a little, I realized that I could not write these same books now—I discovered in them a certain youthfulness and innocence that came from just that, my youth, and my more limited worldview at the time. I'm a very different person and writer than I was then, and it was both enlightening and invigorating to revisit these stories, getting reacquainted with my younger writing self and seeing parts of myself I'd long since forgotten. As part of preserving the context of that worldview, I've chosen to keep this book in its original setting, not updating for technology or other lifestyle changes.

It is with great joy that I present to you *The Guy Next Door* (originally published under the title *Baby Love*) as I intended it to be read. I hope you will enjoy it!

Toni Blake

Chapter One

HOLLY BLAKE STUDIED the twisted black menagerie beneath the hood of her car. She'd never seen such a ridiculous mess of metal and wire. Coiling and curving around itself like a big blackened knot, she thought it could double for some kind of abstract art.

Surely someone could come up with a simpler plan for putting a car together. Although she had to admit she was acquiring a whole new respect for auto mechanics with each passing second.

"I can do this," she said, leaning over the left fender to look down at Emily.

"Gaaaa," Emily replied, frowning.

Holly smiled down at the baby in the pink carrier seat. "Have some faith in Mommy. I can do it. You and I are on our own and we have to start being independent." Then she turned her attention back to the mangled black mess inside the car. "Now, if I were windshield wiper fluid, where in here would I go?"

The longer she studied the car's inner workings, though, the more each part of it started to look like the next. "It's only windshield wiper fluid," she murmured, getting frustrated. "This should be simple."

Guess I should have learned some of these simple things. I should have taken a little responsibility for some of the small duties in my life. But she and Bill had assumed old-fashioned, traditional roles in their marriage—she'd done the cooking and the cleaning, he'd handled the cars and the lawn. And she'd never thought she would need to know where the windshield wiper fluid went. She'd never thought she'd be alone.

The heavy beat of loud rock music suddenly filled Holly's ears, slicing into the calm sounds of late summer suburbia. Glancing up from beneath the hood, she caught sight of a familiar pickup truck cutting a noisy swath down the tree-lined street. She'd quickly learned to recognize her new neighbor's vehicle by sound because no one else in her neighborhood would dare play music that loud.

Although the music blaring from the truck really didn't bother her all that much. In fact, something about it seemed to connect with a long-forgotten part of herself deep down inside, making her feel alive in a way she hadn't since she was a teenager. As she shifted her eyes across the street to find old Mr. Nutter holding his irritated German shepherd by the collar and scowling at the approaching vehicle, she suppressed a grin.

The truck careened into the driveway separated from Holly's by only a small patch of grass and a couple of thin trees, then the music died along with the pickup's engine, restoring peace to the late summer day. She heard her neighbor get out and slam the door, but she was careful to keep her eyes on the twisted black metal and not look up. She wasn't sure why.

Oh yes you are, that long-forgotten, suddenly-alive part of her said.

Shut up, her more conservative self replied.

But she couldn't deny the facts—the alive part of her spoke the truth. She didn't want to look at him because of the way he affected her body.

Every time she saw him, her nipples hardened beneath her bra. And her panties, well…they, too—or, more precisely, what went on inside them—reminded her of what it was like to be young and…*ready*. That was it. Looking at him made her feel ready. For anything. Everything.

So it was better not to look. She was a mother, after all. With a ton of responsibilities, some of which she couldn't even handle on her best days. She had to have priorities or everything would fall to pieces. Well, the parts that hadn't *already* fallen to pieces. She had to hang on to the ones that were still intact.

She leaned over the fender to peer down at Emily again, and this time the baby smiled up at her conspiratorially.

"Don't give me that look, young lady," Holly teased her. "You're way too young to be having those kinds of thoughts. And I'm way too old."

But wait. Twenty-eight was hardly old. *It only feels*

that way.

Getting the call about Bill's car crash when she'd been only three months pregnant had added a few years to her life, she supposed. And having Emily without him, facing parenthood alone, had added a few more. Even this kind of stuff—around the house fix-its and car maintenance—always added at least another one or two. Sometimes it was the little things that dragged a person down. Being both mother and father, caretaker and provider, had begun to wear Holly thin.

But I'm doing fine. "Or at least I would be," she muttered, "if I could figure out where this darn windshield wiper fluid goes."

"Maybe I can help."

The voice was deep. And so were the eyes, when she lifted her gaze to his. Deep and brown and downright hot. Or maybe the hot part was merely an illusion given off by the sweat-soaked white T-shirt that hugged his chest and torso.

He was a construction worker. She'd thought it before, but now she knew for sure. He wore tattered blue jeans and scuffed brown workboots, and his muscular arms bore the kind of tan that only came from working outdoors. His dark hair, wet around the edges, clung to his bronzed skin.

"Sorry," he said. "I didn't mean to scare you."

Okay, speak now. Say something. Anything. "You didn't." She shook her head, probably too vigorously. "I...I...I'm confused."

"I can see that," he said with a smile. Heat filled her veins and she feared she might faint. What had the weatherman said about the temperature today? Eighty degrees? It felt more like a hundred.

"I...don't know anything about cars," she explained, shifting her glance back to the blackened tapestry of the engine. "And I'm...out of wiper stuff."

As he took the plastic jug of blue liquid from her hand, his fingers brushed against hers, and some kind of tremor shook her. *Great—first unbearable heat, now earthquakes.* Although he didn't look too alarmed, so she quickly deduced that the earthquake must just be inside her. *Geez, get hold of yourself.*

"I can take care of that for you," he offered. Reaching into his pocket to pull out a small red bandanna, he used it to unscrew a cap previously invisible to her in the tightly wrapped metal. Then he began to empty the container, the blue liquid flowing smoothly into some dark, hidden area beneath the hood.

When he'd recapped both the windshield wiper fluid and the car's receptacle, he shoved the bandanna back into his pocket and stretched one strong, tan finger toward the black cap under the hood. "See," he explained, pointing. "It's right here, mounted on the fire wall, next to the transmission dipstick."

"Okay," she said, trying to make a mental note. "Thanks." Dare she risk looking up at him again? It seemed a dangerous move. But she really had to—didn't she?—to be polite. So she cautiously lifted her gaze.

"I'm Derek Cassidy," he said.

Unfortunately, his delicious brown eyes had already pinned her in place and again denied her the power of speech. So she simply stared at him.

"I just moved in next door to you a couple of weeks ago."

He motioned over his shoulder and Holly managed a nod.

"And you are?" He leaned slightly forward and asked with a small grin.

Melting. Like butter in the sun. "Holly," she finally sputtered. "Holly Blake."

Derek smiled, flattered at her breathtaken response to him, but maybe not altogether surprised. His father hadn't given him much, but one thing he had passed on to his son was a way with women.

"Well, it's nice to meet you, Holly Blake."

"You, too," she said, finally offering him a smile of her own.

She was pretty when she smiled. Of course, she was also pretty when she *didn't* smile. Which was what had brought him over here in the first place. She hadn't looked much like his type, but arriving home to see her puzzled expression beaming down over the engine of her car had been an invitation he couldn't resist.

"I don't know what I'd have done if you hadn't come over," she added.

"Driven around with dirty windows, I guess."

She blushed. "Yeah, I suppose it wasn't exactly a catastrophe, was it? I'm just not really used to doing these things."

"Husband away on business?" he ventured, mentally crossing his fingers that there *was* no husband.

She bit her lip, then looked uncertainly up at him. "Husband just…away."

Hmm, this was getting interesting. "Away?"

"I'm kind of…widowed," she replied.

Oh crap. Her husband had *died*, and here he was, fishing for information like a schoolboy in heat. "I'm sorry," he rushed.

"It's all right," she said. "It was a year ago. But sometimes it still seems…like yesterday."

Okay, he knew when a woman was sending him a message. If the words didn't plainly say it, the nervous eyes did. She was recently widowed and not ready for romance yet.

Which was probably just as well in the long run. Because his original instincts had been correct—she wasn't his type. Dressed in tailored shorts not meant for doing chores, along with an embroidered summer top tucked tightly in at the waist, it was easy to see that she was a prim and conservative woman.

Not that there was anything wrong with that. But it wasn't his usual fare.

"I'm really sorry," he felt the need to say again. "About your husband."

"I've adjusted," she insisted in a bolder tone that surprised him a little. "I mean, except for times like this, when I'm trying to put in windshield wiper fluid and that sort of thing."

He smiled and nodded. "Well, I'm right next door whenever you need anything," he told her. And he meant it. Even if there wasn't a romance in the works, he was a sucker for a pretty lady in distress. And who knew— maybe eventually she'd decide she wanted to be more than just friends. He thought the confident tone he'd detected in her voice just now might have held a hint of promise he hadn't heard there at first.

"Thanks," she said, now glancing down and suddenly looking almost shy, maybe even delicate in a way.

And the unexpected expression made his heart feel somehow as if it were bending inside his chest.

He quickly shook the sensation off. What the hell was *that*? Well, didn't matter—it was over.

But he still wanted to make sure she understood just how available he was—should the need for help arise. "Anything breaks or falls apart," he said, "I can probably fix it."

Then he reached in his back pocket to fish out his wallet. Opening it, he pulled out a business card—only slightly smudged with dirt—and slid it between her fingers. "Here's my number. If you need me."

She looked down at the card, then back up at him. "You have your own construction company," she said approvingly.

He nodded. He didn't mind anyone being impressed by his achievements. Considering his background, sometimes he was pretty impressed himself. "I started out on my own about five years ago," he told her. "I have a crew of twelve now, and the business seems to keep coming my way."

Her eyes brimmed with warmth. "That's great. I really admire anyone with enough ambition to start their own business."

"Of course," he added with a wink, "there's no charge for neighbors." *Especially pretty ones.* But he wasn't sure she'd want to know that his kindness stemmed partially from that.

She smiled up at him, her green eyes sparkling in the late day sun.

And he smiled back, trying not to turn on the flirtation that came to him so naturally. But it was difficult.

As a small silence grew between them, he suffered a familiar stirring inside. Despite his attempt at an innocent smile, he wanted to get closer to her—that fast. He'd always been a fast mover with girls—he couldn't help it; it was his nature. And now he envisioned himself running his fingers through her hair, long and reddish-blond—strawberry blond, he thought they called that. Then he imagined touching her lips, small and pouty and a color that reminded him of berries.

But whoa. This very nice woman had given him no reason to believe she'd welcome a come-on. And he knew he should leave before his stirrings got the best of him and he ended up looking like a jackass. He turned his attention to her car, where it was safer, and slammed down the hood.

"Thanks again," she told him. "Now I'll be able to see where I'm going when I'm driving to school tomorrow morning."

"School?" he asked.

"I'm a teacher," she explained. "Third grade. School just started last week."

Wow, they hadn't made teachers that pretty when *he* was a kid. Although…being a schoolteacher made her all the more not his type. So again, it was time to go and leave the pretty lady be. "Well," he said, "I'll be seeing you around the neighborhood."

As Holly raised her eyes to his, she bit her lush lower lip in…well, what, from most women, Derek would interpret as a sexy, flirtatious way. *Damn* sexy and flirtatious. He felt it in his gut. And he couldn't help wondering if perhaps he'd been misreading her this whole time.

Maybe she wasn't shying away from men at all. In fact, maybe he was just the thing to take her mind off her late husband. His heart did that bending thing again in his chest—but he tried not to think about that. He'd much rather think about the pretty schoolteacher in the dressy shorts who stood before him looking wistful and almost inviting. He wondered if *he* could teach *her* anything. A smile laced with a bit of lechery came to his lips, but he forced it away. Maybe he would ask her out to dinner. Casually.

"Listen," he began, "if you're not busy—"

"Waaaaaaaa!"

What the hell...? "What's that?" he asked. It had come from the opposite side of the car and it sounded like...a baby.

"That," she said, bending over the fender and hoisting a carrier complete with small child up into her arms, "is my daughter, Emily."

He stood looking down on the baby, completely dumbstruck. It had been there this whole time? And it belonged to her?

"Waaaa! Waaaaa!"

"Oh, now," Holly said, scooping the pastel-clad baby up into her arms and lowering the carrier back to the ground, "What's all the fuss about?"

"Waaaaaaaa!"

Derek couldn't believe how completely calm she seemed despite the baby's ear-splitting screams—they practically sent chills up his spine.

"She gets impatient sometimes when I don't pay attention to her," Holly explained.

And he nodded, not quite sure how to respond.

So he simply watched as she leaned over the baby with wide eyes, cooing until the child's cries began to subside. Then she shifted the baby until she held it nearly upright, its face pointed absently toward him.

"Emily," Holly said, "I would like you to meet our new neighbor, Derek. Derek, this is Emily."

Derek had never been around a baby before, let alone been formally introduced to one. He didn't know what he was supposed to do. "Hi…Emily," he finally said, fearing he sounded awkward. But it *felt* awkward to talk to someone who had no idea what he was saying. In fact, it seemed downright silly.

"Well," Holly said, lifting her eyes back to him, "I suppose we've kept you long enough. You're probably tired after working in the hot sun all day. But we appreciate the assistance with the car."

"Glad I could help you out," he replied.

But in truth, he'd suddenly grown anxious to get away. He was still trying to get over his surprise at finding out the pretty schoolteacher had a baby!

"It was very nice to meet you, Derek," she said then. And he peered down at her face, shocked that her voice had gone velvet-soft and that she was gazing at him with completely sexy eyes.

Were these the eyes of a staid schoolteacher? It didn't seem possible. If she had looked at him like that five minutes ago, he'd definitely have asked her out, tailored shorts or no tailored shorts. But as it was, all he wanted to do was run. And he also wanted her to quit being so pretty and alluring—because it would make the running part much easier.

"You, too," he said, backing away, his eyes glued helplessly to the woman before him.

Yet even as he gazed admiringly at the tempting Holly Blake, his senses taking in all her obvious charms, he still couldn't quit seeing the bigger picture, the picture which had switched him to run mode, the picture that included the baby in her arms.

He'd been right in the first place. She definitely wasn't his type.

HOLLY TWISTED THE knob on the Winnie-the-Pooh mobile above Emily's bed until the Pooh theme song tinkled merrily forth.

She sang along with it, tickling Emily as she lay her on the changing table. "Something about a bear…hmm hmm hmm hmm." Okay, so she didn't exactly remember all the words. She'd have to make a point of learning them by the time Emily could sing.

She unbuttoned her daughter's pale yellow sleeper and extracted the baby's pudgy legs. Then she removed the wet diaper and slid a new one under Emily's behind, fastening the tabs and putting the sleeper back in place. "There you go, punkin," she said, lifting the baby into her arms.

That was when she caught sight of him, out the window. She released a gasp and became aware of her own heartbeat. "Oh God," she murmured. "There he is."

Derek had changed into a pair of frayed khaki cargo shorts and a clean tee, and he padded barefoot through his yard toward the mailbox.

She held the baby up to face the window, then quickly laughed at her own actions. Emily was obviously a little too young right now to see what Holly saw. Noting the boredom in the baby's eyes, which seemed about to close, she lowered Emmy into the baby bed, twisting the mobile once more before the music began to fade. Then she returned to the window. And the man.

Now he'd begun spraying his lawn, a hose in one hand, a drink can in the other. Letting her eyes pore over the same muscles she'd noticed earlier, she experienced a physical reaction—an undeniable fluttering sensation in her panties.

He looked so hard, so tough. She'd have bet there wasn't a soft spot on his entire body. Then she thought of one spot that would be particularly appealing when hard, and another tremor shook her.

"This isn't like me," she said, casting a glance at her daughter. But Emily had already conked out, and it was just as well. It felt weird having such unwholesome feelings with her six-month-old right next to her.

And still, she couldn't *deny* those feelings—they were pumping through her veins like electricity, making her more aware of her own body than she'd been since giving birth.

She'd never been attracted to that kind of a man before. Tough, rugged men—bad boy types—had never really appealed to her like they had to so many other girls. She'd always been sensible, dating the smart boys: the college-bound debating champion, the winner of the science fair. And she'd never expected to be attracted to a man because of his body, because of his muscles and his tan, because of the beads of sweat that clung to his skin.

Maybe the tough boys had scared her when she was

younger.

And now apparently that fear had passed. In a big way.

But hey, hormones are hormones. And there's a first time for everything. So this is really no big deal.

Which was good. Because there was no time for a man in her life right now anyway. It was difficult enough being at school all day, grading papers at night, and carving out some quality time to spend with Emily in between. So Derek Cassidy would simply be her neighbor, her fix-it man, her fantasy.

Wait a minute. *Fantasy?*

"I can't want this guy," she murmured.

She really couldn't. It was totally illogical and unrealistic. And talk about your bad timing.

But she *did* want him.

And that quick, she feared it was something over which she had no control.

Chapter Two

———— ∽∽ ————

HOLLY LAY IN bed thinking about raging hormones. Or, to be honest with herself, she was *trying* to think about raging hormones, trying to attribute her uncharacteristic feelings to that—but inside it felt like much more than simple hormones.

But hormones always feel like more than hormones. And that's the trouble with hormones.

Drifting into half-sleep, she saw a cloudy vision of the two of them. She envisioned herself inviting him in, offering him a cup of coffee, sitting with him at the kitchen table, chatting and getting to know him…

But that quickly grew boring, so her mind raced feverishly ahead and she soon saw herself peeling off his clothes and him doing the same to her.

Piece by piece, thread by thread, revealing her soft white skin and his hard, tanned muscles.

In the vision, his skin was shiny, like he'd just come in from the hot sun, like he'd been working very strenuously. She imagined touching every inch of his hard, glistening body, exploring the muscles in his arms and chest, caressing his shoulders, running her fingers though his thick, dark hair.

But wait, the mother inside her suddenly said, jolting her awake, *where is Emily through all of this?*

Emily is in a deep, deep sleep, the dreamy and alive part of her replied.

Not that that was necessarily realistic, but neither was any of this.

Forgetting that, she rolled over and pulled the sheets up around her, and then she got back to the good part—him. She imagined how his sweat-salty kisses would taste on her lips, then how they would feel as he moved his mouth slowly down her body, to her neck, her breasts, her stomach, then below. "Oh my," she whispered into the darkness.

By the time Holly got out of bed the next morning, she was exhausted. She'd spent the entire night dreaming about hot sex with her new neighbor. Which would explain why her cotton pajamas were damp with perspiration. She shook her head and reached for her robe, ready to put such silliness behind her.

"Morning, Em," she said a few minutes later, reaching into the baby bed to extract her daughter.

"Aaaaa." Emily looked bright-eyed and chipper this morning, making her envious. She, for one, had slept lousy. And it was all Derek Cassidy's fault.

She carried Emily toward the kitchen, thinking about how silly it was to lose sleep over this guy. She barely knew the man, after all. She lowered the baby into the bouncer seat on the kitchen floor, then moved to the counter to start fixing a bottle.

"Enh," Emily said, her brows furrowing.

A moment later Holly slipped the fresh bottle into Emily's mouth and watched her daughter eat breakfast. As Emily sucked on the bottle, Holly focused on the softness of her daughter's cheek, the tiny fingers that clutched at the plastic container, the eyes that closed in complete satiation.

Up until yesterday, such things were enough to completely occupy Holly's mind. And she thought she'd liked it better that way.

Well, maybe her *mind* had liked it better that way. It was simpler, after all. There was no challenge in it, no fear—only the contentment of motherhood. When Bill had died, she'd told herself that was all she'd need to get through life from now on, and she'd believed it.

So why was she still thinking about Derek? Because…that's where her body entered the picture. Her body seemed to like thinking about him a *lot*. Which was troubling. After all, she'd literally lost sleep over the man. And she didn't even know him. This seemed unhealthy.

"I never felt like that about Bill," she mused, mumbling.

"Aaaaa," Emily stopped eating and looked up to say.

"I wasn't talking to you, young lady," Holly told her. "Now be a good baby and drink your breakfast."

After reaching into the pantry for a box of cereal, she poured some flakes into a bowl and dropped a couple of slices of bread into the toaster. She ate quickly, still standing at the kitchen counter, then carried Emily's baby seat into the bedroom with her. The hardest part of the day was coming, and the familiar gnawing that began to eat away at her stomach was actually enough to take her mind off her sexy new neighbor. She worked not to let Emily see her dismay.

Digging in the closet, she pulled out a casual dress and slipped it off the hanger, then laid out shoes, undies and a bra.

"Mommy will be right back," she said to Emily before heading to take a quick shower and returning to the bedroom to dress.

She chatted playfully to her daughter as she got ready for work, telling her to be a good girl for Miss Carol today and promising her lots of stories and songs and other fun things that night after Holly retrieved her from daycare.

But after being rewarded with a big, happy grin, Holly's heart sank. How many more of those grins would she miss today? How many funny faces or silly noises might Emily make in her absence?

Dropping Emmy off each morning was the most difficult thing she had ever been forced to adapt to. And when she'd told Derek Cassidy she was adjusting to life without Bill, she definitely hadn't been talking about *this* part.

When she and Bill had decided to have a baby, they'd agreed that Holly would stay home and be the perfect mother to their child. Of course, everything had changed since then. And now she had no choice but to take Emily to daycare every morning and struggle through the day at school just waiting for the moment they could be together again.

Holly knew that some mothers handled such arrangements well, conforming to the busy working-mom lifestyle. But so far she hadn't personally found the secret to success. Many mornings she rushed from the daycare center back out to her car only to sit there and cry. She often felt the urge to march right back in for Emily and take them both back home, responsibilities be damned.

But the harsh reality was that they needed money to live. So she always found a way to pull herself together and go on to school, hoping Emily was getting enough attention and at the same time hoping that she wasn't missing her child's first words or efforts to crawl, and living all day for the moment when she would see her again.

Holly put on a pair of earrings and pulled her long hair back in a loose chignon. Then she dressed Emily in a pair of pink overalls with a lavender T-shirt underneath, packed a diaper bag, and set off for Miss Carol's. Another day, another heartache.

She thought out loud as she carried the baby out to the car. "Maybe we'll cook out on the grill tonight, Em." Then added hopefully, "And maybe we'll see that nice new neighbor again."

THE SOUNDS OF hammers and nails filled the hot, sultry air as Derek stood back to survey the framing job his men worked on.

He swabbed perspiration from his face with a blue bandanna, then shoved it back into his pocket. And reaching in again, he found the old watch he carried to keep track of time on the job sites. The cloudy face read 3:30.

"Hey, guys!" he yelled, getting their attention and replacing the sounds of hammers with silence. "Knock off for the day."

The men were hard workers, each and every one of them, but they looked happy enough to start packing up their tools.

"I'm late for an appointment," he told them, "but I'll see everybody in the morning."

Then he hopped in his pickup and started the engine. He turned on the radio, cranking the volume as usual, then drove from the dirt lot out onto the street and set off toward the office of Mr. Greely, the lawyer handling his aunt's estate.

Most of the estate had been settled—there were only a few loose ends left to tie up. And he'd be glad to get it behind him. As much as he appreciated Aunt Marie leaving him her house, he was finding it more difficult to live there so far than he'd expected—it felt strange to be surrounded by her things and know she was no longer around. And as much as he appreciated her faith in him to be the executor of the will, it was hard to hand out her cherished possessions to her friends and loved ones without continually feeling the loss.

If Aunt Marie hadn't taken me in when she did, where would I be now? He shook his head—the prospects weren't promising. Then he made a mental note to pick up some fresh flowers for the cemetery.

Just as he decided to turn his mind to more pleasant thoughts, an old song came on the radio—Van Halen singing about beautiful girls. It made him think of Holly Blake with that lovely red-blond hair and that soft, shy smile. What a pretty picture she created in his head.

But then he remembered—Holly Blake was more than just a woman. Holly Blake was a package deal. She had a baby.

Not that he had anything *against* babies. He just hadn't expected it. He guessed he'd hoped she'd be completely free, with no ties—like him. A baby *had* to limit the amount of fun you could have with a woman.

Wow, does this make me a piece of shit? After all, anyone would think he was an ogre for having bad thoughts against an innocent, helpless baby.

Still, late night feedings and diaper changings just weren't his idea of a great time. Hell, they weren't even his idea of a *good* time. Any way he looked at it, it would have to be a drag.

DEREK PULLED INTO his driveway a little after seven. The meeting had taken quite a while, but they'd finally settled Aunt Marie's estate. Which was good. He didn't want to think about it anymore. Too depressing.

When he climbed out of the truck, he found the warm air filled with the scent of hamburgers on a grill. One of the neighbors was cooking out. Nice night for it, too. The temperature was perfect and the day's humidity had completely dissipated. He drank in the aroma, sorry to remember that the only food awaiting him in the house were cold cuts in the fridge.

Once inside, he took a quick shower, glad to rid himself of the day's grime. Then he changed into shorts and a T-shirt and made himself a big sandwich.

When he checked the mail a little while later, scents of the cookout still wafted through the air. He strolled barefoot back through the cool grass of the front yard, thumbing through envelopes and store flyers—and he'd just stepped up onto the porch, reaching for the door handle, when he glanced down to see a little gray kitten peering up at him.

He drew back slightly. "Who do *you* belong to?" he asked, studying the little furball.

The kitten blocked his entry into the house, so he nudged it aside with his foot. In response, the little cat looked up at him and released a hearty meow.

When he opened the door, the kitten made a lunge to get inside, but he quickly stopped the cat's progress, once again pushing him back with his foot. "Oh-h-ho no you don't," he said, and then managed to shut the screen door in the kitten's face, keeping him out.

After grabbing a soft drink from the fridge, then settling on Aunt Marie's couch in front of the TV, he found himself wondering where that kitten had come from—if it belonged to someone and just gotten out, gotten lost. Maybe it belonged to Holly next door? She seemed like the kind of person who would have a cat, who would *like* a cat. After all, she liked babies, and the two seemed similar. They needed to be fed and kept warm and cared for. He gave a little shudder, perishing the thought.

Not that he usually spent a lot of time worrying about stray cats. Cats wandered through job sites all the time and he generally paid them no attention. But he wasn't used to having a teeny tiny one meowing up at him on his front porch.

He found himself channel surfing then, seeking something to occupy his mind. He wondered what Holly was doing right now. How long had she and her husband been married before he'd died? Was she still in love with him? What did she look like when she was sleeping?

What did she look like when she was sleeping? Where on earth had *that* come from? He didn't know the answer and he wasn't sure he wanted to find out. It wasn't like him to let a woman invade his mind without his permission. He shifted uncomfortably on the couch.

Bored with everything on TV, he turned it off. Normally, he might sit outside and with his soda and enjoy the weather on a nice night like this. Or mow the lawn or start the repairs on the back deck that he'd been meaning to get to. But something was keeping him inside the house tonight—and that something was obviously Holly Blake.

But wait. Correction. Holly Blake's baby. As instantly smitten as he'd apparently become with the woman—she was on his mind right now, after all, for no good reason—he just wasn't ready to date someone with a built-in family. So, as much as he hated to admit it to himself, he must be avoiding her.

Padding to the kitchen to toss his drink can in the garbage, a small scratching noise drew his attention toward the old sliding door that led to the deck. The gray furball he'd met on the front porch had now moved to the back, and it had caught sight of him through the glass. He grimaced at the cat.

That was when it began climbing up the screen until it hung from it, attached by all four paws. Hmm— maybe the cat didn't belong to Holly, after all, or anyone else on the street, or it would probably be *there*, bothering *them*, hanging on *their* screen. "How did I get so lucky that you would choose *me* from an entire neighborhood?" he groused at the kitten through the screen door.

"Meowwwww."

If he was reading this correctly—and he didn't really know cats, so maybe he wasn't—he thought the dumb little thing was stuck in place, a couple feet off the deck, and now getting panicky. So he sighed and took mercy on it, sliding the screen door open, reaching around, and using one hand to—as carefully as possible—detach the cat's claws from his screen. Then he lowered it to the deck and watched it scuttle into the house before he could even think about stopping it.

"Great," he muttered. He hadn't known cats were so pushy.

But whatever. He supposed having it inside was better than having his screen door sliced to ribbons.

He was about to pull the door shut again when he caught a glimpse of Holly Blake through the arborvitae trees that separated their backyards. She sat a table on her patio eating a hamburger, and the baby sat perched next to her on the table in her carrier thing. Holly wore a sleeveless blouse and her hair was pulled back from her face. She had the most incredible green eyes. He couldn't see them from that distance, of course, but he was remembering them from their encounter yesterday.

When he realized that his heart was bending in his chest again, he was almost tempted to quit avoiding her and go on over. He could take the cat and ask if it was hers. Or—hell, he didn't need a pretense to approach a pretty woman—he could be honest and tell her he'd seen her outside and just wanted to say hi.

But then he heard a bubbly, gurgling noise erupt from the baby on the table. He silently watched and waited—in anticipation, and maybe even a sense of prediction—until the noise expanded into a full cry, sending a shot of tension racing up his spine.

"There, there, Em," Holly said, abandoning her hamburger to rise from her seat and peer down on the baby.

But the baby kept crying and Derek just felt thankful he wasn't any closer.

"Well, aren't you the fussy one tonight?" Holly remarked.

But he didn't hear any more, because that was when he pulled his head back inside and slid the door shut. Going over there had been a bad idea and he was glad he hadn't acted on it.

He turned in his kitchen to see a certain gray kitten pawing at the garbage can—where a milk container he'd emptied this morning protruded from the top. He let out a sigh, but figured it wouldn't kill him to be nice to the silly little thing. The sound of claws on hard plastic made him say, "All right already—calm down."

Opening the refrigerator, he poured some milk into a small bowl and set it on the kitchen floor. The kitten practically attacked it, lapping at the milk furiously.

"But don't get too comfortable," he told the cat. "This isn't a permanent thing."

Though after watching the kitten lick the bowl dry, he felt unusually generous for reasons he didn't understand, so much so that he even found a can of tuna in a cabinet, opened it up, and spooned it into the bowl.

"But that's it, cat," he warned. "After this, you're outta here."

When the kitten had finished the tuna, Derek picked it up and carried it to the back door. He was about to lower the cat to the wooden deck, mentally preparing to close the door quickly so he couldn't scamper back in— when he caught sight of Holly and Emily again. Now Holly held the baby and sang to her.

"Hush little baby, don't say a word, mama's gonna buy you a mockingbird. If that mockingbird don't sing…"

Despite himself, he stood transfixed, watching and listening to her pretty voice. Her song had quieted the baby. And he couldn't deny how lovely she looked just sitting there cradling the child in her arms, like some kind of wholesome vision almost too pristine for his eyes. His heart was starting the bending thing again and—

"Meow."

"Hey," Derek said, looking down at the kitten in his left hand—it had been an unusually loud *meow*. "Knock it off." Was the cat trying to draw attention to him or something?

"Meowww," the kitten bawled again.

"That's it, cat. Free ride's over."

And with that, Derek plunked the kitten to the deck and slid the door firmly shut. Then he closed the vertical blinds so the cat wouldn't be able to see him and he wouldn't be able to see the cat.

Ridiculous. First being taken in by a pretty woman, and then a cat. You must be losing your edge, Cassidy.

DEREK STEPPED OUT of the shower the next morning and threw on a pair of jeans and a clean red T-shirt. Grabbing his wallet and a clean bandanna from his dresser drawer, he shoved both into his pocket. Then he snatched a stale donut from a box he'd picked up a couple days earlier and quickly downed it, followed by a chug of milk from the jug he'd opened last night for the cat.

The memory made him feel smug. *Haven't even thought about that cat, or that woman, since I shut the door on both of them last night.* "Must be getting your edge back," he murmured.

Then he rushed out the front door.

And without warning, the small gray kitten leapt wildly onto his leg, digging into the denim with its claws to end up hanging suspended near Derek's knee.

"Hey!"

He shook his head, getting past the short-lived alarm of the moment, then reached down to detach the cat. The damn thing had come out of nowhere and he absently wondered how long it had been waiting outside his front door to ambush him.

He stepped off the porch, holding the cat out in front of his face and looking into its eyes. "We've gotta quit meeting like this," he said, arching one eyebrow in warning.

"Meow," the kitten said with a helpless, desperate

look on its tiny face.

Derek could only sigh. "Look, cat," he said, "it's nothing personal, but I'm not a cat guy." Kind of like he wasn't a baby guy. Some things just didn't mix. Oil and water. Him and cats. "So you're gonna have to shop for a new owner somewhere else. I'd suggest the lady next door. I have a feeling she'd like you."

"Good morning!"

Lifting his gaze, Derek glanced across the lawn to see none other than Holly Blake wearing a long bathrobe, hints of some kind of nightgown peeking from it, and toting a baby on her hip. She stooped to pick up her newspaper as she smiled at him, her face framed by beautifully unbrushed hair. His first impression? That any woman who looked that good first thing in the morning would be nice to wake up next to.

"Good morning," he replied, still holding the cat out in front of him.

"You have a cat," she said, that dazzling smile sparkling on him, and he could have sworn her eyes had lit up when she'd spoken. He knew it. She was a cat person.

"Uh, yeah," he heard himself reply uncertainly, "I...have a cat." He took a few steps toward her yard, moving instinctively in that direction without really ever having decided to, the cat still held out in front of him.

She stepped closer, too. "What's its name?"

Hmm. That was a damn good question. "I just call it...cat."

As she tilted her pretty head and bit her berry-colored lip, Derek felt himself being sucked back under yet again. It wasn't like not being able to breathe, but more like just not having full control over himself—his actions, decisions.

"A cat really needs a better name than that," she told him.

"Well," he said on impulse, "maybe you can help me think of one."

But wait a minute. What was he doing here? Flirting with her? The woman was holding a baby, for God's sake. Where was his head?

Inside her nightgown, apparently.

Although he couldn't see much of it other than its fairly high neck and flowered print, he was totally attracted to her in it, which should have surprised him but didn't. Her gorgeousness evidently overrode a grandma-style nightgown.

Feeling awkward, he trained his eyes back on the cat. "This is all your fault," he muttered. Then he lifted his eyes to Holly again.

"Why don't you come in," she suggested, "and we can think of a name for your cat over some coffee."

Chapter Three

*T*HANKS, BUT *I can't.*
    I'm late for work.
Gotta run.
Maybe another time.

Those were all the things he said in his mind. But from his mouth, he heard only one little word. "Sure."

Shit—must be losing my edge again. That was fast.

And then his feet got in on the act, too, following Holly, cat in hand, toward her front door.

But this would be a good wake-up call. After all, a few minutes with a baby would get him back in his right mind. And then he could get over this little infatuation and get on with his life. And maybe he could even palm the cat off on Holly in the process.

By the time he was inside her house, she was returning the baby to a playpen in the dining room, just beyond the living room.

"Have a seat," she said, motioning toward the table there. "I'll pour the coffee." Then she disappeared through the kitchen doorway.

Derek awkwardly complied, he and his new cat sitting down near the baby.

"Goooooo," the baby said, looking up at him.

He glanced down at the tiny person, then back to the cat, who now clung to his chest. He simply shook his head. How had he ended up like this?

"Emily's saying hi to you," Holly informed him from the kitchen.

He swallowed, then looked back down at the baby. She wore a light green one-piece summer thing. "Hi," he said, feeling completely ridiculous. What did you say to a baby, after all? Since they couldn't understand you, it seemed like a waste to talk at all.

When Holly came to the table carrying two cups of coffee, Derek withdrew his gaze from the baby and turned it on her mother, who—one more close-up glance assured him—definitely *would* be great to wake up next to. Her eyes were bright and clear, her porcelain skin flawless, and her unkempt hair gave the impression of something wild hiding within the prim schoolteacher.

"Thanks," he said as she set a steaming mug before him.

"So," she said, taking the chair adjacent to his, "your cat needs a name."

"Well," he said with a grin, "I thought just 'cat' was good enough, but now you've informed me that I'm misguided."

"Can I hold him?" she asked. "And is it a 'him'?"

"Sure," he said in answer to the first question.

"And…I'm not sure," he replied a bit awkwardly to the second.

"New cat, I take it?" she asked in response, eyebrows raised.

And he nodded, feeling stupid for telling her the cat was his, yet not even knowing if it was a boy or a girl.

Holly stood and reached out for the cat, which still clung to his chest. Long tendrils of her strawberry blond hair hung near Derek's face and her nearness made his heart begin to pound in his chest. She slid her soft hands over his where he held onto the kitten, the touch electrifying. Then he pulled his grip gently away, releasing the cat to her grasp.

She lowered back into her chair, cooing and hugging the ball of fur, but Derek's mind still lingered on the touch of her hand and the soft, musky scent that had wafted over him when she'd leaned near.

"You can always go with a typical cat name," she informed him, looking down into the cat's eyes. "You know—Fluffy, Puffy, something like that."

But the idea of owning something named Fluffy didn't appeal. If he had to own a cat, it had to have a more solid name. "What are my other options?"

"Well," she said, suddenly flipping the cat over on its back, "it would help to find out if it's a boy or a girl."

Something about watching the woman study his new cat's genitals was a little unnerving, although he didn't really know why. But he looked away until she was done.

"It's a boy," she announced as merrily as a delivery

room doctor on TV.

Derek nodded.

"So you could really go with any boy name you like, too," she added.

Any boy name he liked. Which fell under big the umbrella of things he'd never thought about in his life.

"Why don't you just pick one for me?" he suggested, offering an indulgent grin.

So it surprised him when she replied, "No, you have to pick it yourself. After all, I wouldn't have let anyone else name Emily."

"This is a little different," he reminded her, glancing down at the baby, who stuck out her lower lip. "This is a cat."

"Still, he's *yours*," she explained simply, putting it all back on him. Which maybe would have felt a little more logical to him if he'd actually *chosen* to have a cat. "I have a book of baby names I can lend you if you like."

Derek released an uncomfortable laugh, then took a sip of coffee. "That won't be necessary," he said. "I mean, I'm sure I can come up with something."

"How long have you had this cat?" she asked then.

Uh-oh, he'd been nabbed. A hint of embarrassment bit at him. "Since…last night," he admitted.

"Is he a stray?"

"I guess. He came to my door and wouldn't leave me alone. Why do you ask?"

She smiled and flashed her pretty eyes at him. "Well, I just noticed that he's kind of dirty."

Glancing down then, he suddenly realized that she was right—some of the cat's gray had come off on his shirt.

"I think that underneath," she told him, "this kitten is white."

He was stunned. And he immediately reached out his hands. "Here, let me take him back. I don't want him to get you dirty."

But she just laughed, assuring him, "It's all right."

"Really," he insisted anyway. And he reached for the cat just as she rose toward him, and the back of his hand bumped her breast. He retreated immediately and so did she. "Sorry," he whispered awkwardly.

Then she leaned forward again just as he reached out a second time, and his hand brushed her softness once more. Everything inside him trembled as the sensation struck him—it was like velvet under silk. And this time, he felt the reaction in his pants.

Her cheeks colored with discomfort as she held the cat out to him yet again, her hands extended far from her chest on this attempt. "Let's try it like this," she said.

He deftly snatched the dirty kitten away from her and they both sank back into their chairs, eyes cast downward. Geez, what a clod he was. Not normally, but with this woman, every move he'd made this morning had left him feeling clumsy. He only hoped he hadn't embarrassed her too badly.

He finally glanced up at her from beneath a guarded brow. And when he thought he saw the hint of a smile flicker on her lips, he daringly offered up a small grin. And, to his great relief, they were soon laughing at their own awkwardness.

As their laughter faded, Derek followed an instinct, playfully reminding her, "I thought you invited me over to help name my cat."

"I did," she replied, looking a little defensive, yet maybe flirtatious, too.

"Well, you just offered me a name book and told me I was on my own," he pointed out. "What kind of help is that?"

Her face colored pink again, but this time Derek liked it. He gazed boldly into her pretty green eyes, waiting for her answer.

"Okay," she said softly. "Maybe I didn't really invite you over to help you name your cat."

Huh. He hadn't seen that coming.

He tilted his head slightly and kept his eyes locked on hers. Was it just him, or was there suddenly some strange, electrical current passing between them? Something that felt tense, yet…sensual. "Then what did you invite me over for?"

She looked sheepish and let her gaze fall to the table. "Um, would you believe me if I told you that something broke and I need you to fix it?"

He answered without hesitation, voice low. "No."

Now she lifted her eyes to his face, making his heart pump faster while he waited for her to tell him what he'd already figured out. "Okay—maybe I just wanted…to see you again."

Her words left him stunned. He'd figured it out, yes, but he hadn't really expected her to say it. Not so plainly. So he simply let his gaze consume her for a moment more, before finally telling her, "I'm glad."

"You are?" she whispered.

"Yeah," he said softly. "Because I wanted to see you again, too."

She smiled in the same shy way as when they'd stood next to her car yesterday. Something about that smile had totally turned him on then, and it was turning him on again now, too.

So he followed his next impulse, since it turned out impulses were actually working for him here better than he'd realized up to now. "Can I take you out to dinner? Tonight?"

But as she glanced down, releasing a heavy sigh, he rethought the impulse thing, his heart sinking. He wasn't sure why, but the wind had clearly been let out of her sails. "Derek," she began, "I would really love to, but I can't."

Okay. Regroup. "Tomorrow night then?"

Yet her expression didn't change. "I'm afraid it's not that easy."

"Why not?" he asked. Hadn't she just said she'd wanted to see him again? So what was the problem? He tried to think the whole thing through. "I mean, is it...too soon or something? Since...since your hus-band..." Shit, he didn't know how to phrase it.

Thankfully, though, he didn't have to keep trying, since she shook her head and said, "No, it's not that. It's Emily. After leaving her all day to go to work, I just don't feel right about leaving her at night, too."

"Oh," he murmured, wishing he could hide his disappointment. Wishing even more that he hadn't been so affected by her confession of wanting to see him again. It had felt like he'd just been given a giant gift, or been paid an incredible compliment; it had felt like the first taste of a requited crush in adolescence. Only he wasn't an adolescent. And he didn't enjoy suddenly feeling like one. Especially upon having that gift snatched away almost as soon as it had been given.

"I'm sure that's hard for you to understand, not having any children," Holly went on. "But Emily is my first priority and I have to think of her needs before my own."

Her words left Derek at a loss for what to say. She had him on an emotional roller coaster—first she wanted to see him and then she didn't have time. He supposed he had to admire her commitment to her baby, but why had she bothered expressing interest in him then?

Despite her admission, he couldn't help wondering if maybe she'd just changed her mind. Maybe inviting him in for coffee had been a trial run. Maybe he hadn't passed the test. Maybe the baby was a convenient excuse. So it was time to cut his losses.

"Well," he said, "I should go. Thanks for the coffee." He drained his cup and got to his feet, his cat in his hand.

"Wait," she said, rising as well.

"What?" he asked.

He watched as she pulled in her breath. "Maybe you could...come over and grill out," she suggested cautiously.

Derek immediately dropped a smug glance in the baby's direction and hoped Holly hadn't noticed. And, at the same time, he felt like someone had given him a parachute just before he'd crashed to the ground.

On one hand, maybe he should be running in the opposite direction from a woman who didn't seem to know exactly what she wanted. But on the other hand was how gorgeous she was and how much she'd stayed on his mind since they'd met.

"All right," he said. "Tonight?"

She nodded.

"Seven o'clock?"

She nodded again and he couldn't help but smile. His heart was bending again, bending and twisting itself into a pretzel inside his chest.

Baby or no baby, looked like he was having dinner with Holly Blake tonight.

HOLLY FAIRLY FLOATED into the bedroom, the handle of Emily's carrier looped over her arm like an Easter basket. She set the carrier on her bed, then scooped her daughter up into her arms, twirling her in a circle. "Our new neighbor is coming over to dinner tonight, Em!" How incredible!

A few minutes later, she shed her robe and gown and stepped into the shower. Normally, the morning shower was like torture to her waking body, but today she felt fresh and alive, and ready. Yes, ready. Just like the music he listened to so loudly, Derek's very presence created that same sense of anticipation and excitement inside her. She lathered the soap over her arms and shoulders as the invigorating water blasted down on her skin.

When she'd grilled out last night, she'd hoped maybe he'd wander over, and silly as it was, when there'd been no sign of him, she'd even gone so far as to start concocting stories in her mind. Like that it must mean he had no interest in her whatsoever. Or maybe he was even out on a date. And when she'd seen him outside this morning, instinct had combined with desire and simply taken over.

She'd felt bold inviting him in for coffee, but it had seemed so easy and had progressed so much like her fantasy. And yes, she'd almost blown it there for a minute—almost let her motherly urges shove all her *other* urges back into hiding—but in the end she'd pulled herself together and made something happen! She stepped out of the shower already thinking about progressing to the peeling-off-the-clothes part of her lurid little vision.

But wait. Wrapping a thick towel around herself, she stopped, bit her lower lip. *I'm getting way ahead of myself here.* So he had brushed up against her breast today. Twice. Even so, both times had clearly been unintentional. And a couple of unintentional connections like that didn't mean he wanted *her* with the same intensity that she wanted *him*.

Padding to the bedroom, she released a long sigh. Unintentional or not, the incredible sensations had reminded her of the fire that could burn in her soul, the fire that *had* once burned there, long ago, before marriage and having a baby and grown-up life. She knew some women kept right on feeling those desires and sensations, through everything—but for her, they had faded into the background and other important things had taken over her life.

When his accidental touch had initially occurred, she'd been mortified and had actually wanted to crawl under the table for a moment—she was so glad they had been able to laugh about it in the end. And even as they'd laughed together, even as she'd pretended it was nothing, she'd been enveloped in remembering the velvety contact with his hand.

Was it possible for her to be a mature adult and still have that fire, that readiness that had so consumed her these past couple of days? Could she find the balance between the fear she felt in response to her own emotions and the heat that coursed through her veins?

"This isn't like me," she murmured to herself, stepping back in the bedroom where her daughter waited quietly.

Glancing down at the baby, Holly found twinkling eyes and a sweet smile. She reached out and gently tweaked Emily's tummy through her summer playsuit, making her laugh. "Aaaaa."

But her early morning escapade with Derek had made her late, so she had to hurry. Reaching in the closet, she yanked out the first dress she laid her hand on and rushed to get ready.

She'd figured she'd meet other men and start dating again *eventually*, but she hadn't expected it now. Just like she hadn't expected all this readiness. It had just shown up, out of the clear blue.

And she wasn't sure it was a good time to start dating again, especially not with a guy who could do such delicious things to her with just a glance. She was still trying to get her life in order, after all, and she knew that this would more than likely just complicate things. Feeling confused as she buttoned up the pale yellow dress, she stopped and looked at Emily.

If only Emily were older—old enough to talk, and to have opinions. The baby tilted her head and said, "Enh," as if to remind Holly that she couldn't.

Wouldn't it be nice, though, if Emmy could give her some hint on what to do about Derek. After all, what concerned Holly concerned Emily, too. Holly would never go out with any guy she thought Emily didn't approve of. She would never place her own happiness before her little girl's.

Emily peered up at her with eyes that had just recently become hazel and Holly couldn't help smiling down into them. Was it okay to want this man, another man besides Bill? Another man besides Emily's father? And was this the right time—*now,* when she was already overwhelmed with so many responsibilities?

She sighed, wishing she had the answers. But for now, they remained a mystery.

DEREK PUT ON one his better pairs of jeans and a dark T-shirt. Looking in the bathroom mirror, he brushed his hair, thinking it needed a trim. Not that he ever *usually* thought he needed a trim—he *usually* let his hair grow until it started bothering him. He only thought he needed a trim tonight because he wanted Holly to think he was a nice guy.

"I *am* a nice guy," he said, looking down at his nameless cat, who stood watching him from the doorway. "After all, I adopted *you.*"

Of course, he'd only adopted the cat to make Holly think he was a nice guy. So maybe the act cancelled itself out.

He couldn't remember a time when he'd changed his behavior simply to impress a woman. And he didn't know what was so bad about his real self that he felt the need to cover it up.

He just wasn't as conservative as she seemed to be. He took life as it came and didn't worry over how long his hair was or if he had a clean pair of socks to wear the next day.

"I *am* a nice guy," he said to the mirror.

He wondered if she'd ever dated anyone like him before. He wondered what she would think if she knew about his family—or lack thereof, about the way he'd grown up. A nice woman like her in her dressy shorts and high-necked nightgown—she'd probably be horrified to hear about his youth.

But he'd changed since then. With Aunt Marie's guidance and a little ambition, he'd left his past behind. Now, at thirty-one, he thought he'd finally turned into a pretty nice guy.

"*I am a nice guy*," he insisted once more.

"Meow," the cat said, as if in protest.

What on earth was he doing going over there for dinner anyway? Let alone worrying about making a good impression. Just because the baby hadn't screamed her head off this morning didn't change anything—he still wasn't a baby kind of guy and he had no intentions of becoming one. He might be able to adjust his image by dressing a little nicer than usual and getting a haircut, but that didn't change who he was inside.

"And don't think I'm becoming a cat guy, either," he said, pointing a finger at the dirty kitten.

He checked his watch and discovered it was only 6:30. And he wasn't about to show up early—he didn't want to look eager. Especially considering the baby— that baby might make this a very short-lived romance, and there was no need to give Holly the impression this was going to be a big deal. Gorgeous or not.

He glanced once again at the still-gray kitten. "Maybe I should try to clean you up," he said. It wasn't so much that he cared about *his* house or *his* clothes, but if the cat was gonna be visiting next door, he didn't want it making a mess.

So he bent down and raked the kitten up off the floor—and with his other hand, he ruffled the cat's long fur. Dust flew and he sneezed. "Where have you been living? In a cave?"

He ruffled the kitten's fur some more to send a large amount of gray dust floating up into the air. But it was easy to see that there was more dirt on the cat than a simple rumpling of fur was gonna get rid of. And besides, he had gotten sort of curious as to what the cat would look like in white.

Lowering the kitten onto the top of the clothes hamper, he turned toward the tub and started running a bath. Then he rummaged under the sink and found some bubble bath left from Aunt Marie. Careful to make the water not too cold and not too hot, he let the bubbly pool get a few inches deep.

Pleased with himself, he then lifted the cat from the hamper and gently placed him in the tub. "Get ready, buddy—here it comes."

But when the cat's paws touched the water, it screeched and shot straight into the air, the claws on each paw extended! Water splashed and white soap suds flew, plopping on the toilet, on the floor, and on Derek. After it landed with a plop, it yowled again and tried wildly to clamber up the side of the old porcelain bathtub.

"What the hell is wrong with you?" he asked, grabbing the cat who kept clawing like a maniac at the tub's steep side, then immersing it back into the water.

"Hey, ow—stop that, damn it!" Derek yelled as the cat now clawed madly at his arm instead. "I mean it!" Too bad if the cat didn't like baths—he was gonna get him clean one way or the other.

With that thought in mind, he reached his other hand into the suds that remained in the tub and scrubbed the cat's back. The cat yowled and scratched at him some more, but having come this far, he was determined to get the job done.

After a couple of minutes, the kitten finally calmed down and let Derek wash him, but his little body remained tense and stiff and angry in Derek's grasp.

Of course, when he turned the water back on and held the cat under the faucet to rinse him, World War III broke out all over again, Derek battling the cat.

When the kitten was finally rinsed, Derek grabbed a towel with his free hand and scooped him into it. After mushing him around in the terrycloth for a minute, he set the towel down and watched the wet cat go streaking from the bathroom in search of someplace safe.

"Hey," Derek said in amazement, "you really *are* white."

HOLLY CHECKED HER appearance in the mirror. Shorts and a summery, pastel top were a nice, casual switch from "teacherwear". She'd removed the barrette she'd worn to school that day, as well, letting her long hair fall around her face.

Next she took a look at Emily, lifting her out of her swing where she'd fallen asleep. "Wake up, Em," she said.

Emily had spit up on her mint green sunsuit today at daycare, so Holly had changed her into another cool, sleeveless outfit, this one featuring white poodles adorned with pink bows. "You look pretty, Emily," Holly told her. Then she held her daughter up to let her peer into the mirror. "See how pretty you look."

"Enh," Emily said disinterestedly, glancing away.

"Well, someday you'll really care about this stuff," Holly told her. "I promise."

Emily swung her head around and pointed at her stuffed Eeyore, who lay on his side on the couch. "Aaaaaa," she said.

When the doorbell rang a few minutes later, Holly, Emily, and Eeyore greeted Derek at the door and Holly was immediately taken with how good he looked. It was an entirely different feeling than she got from seeing him after a day's work. When he was decked out in construction gear and sweat, she could think of nothing but heat. Of the most searing kind. But looking at him now, nearly drowning in the deep chocolate hue of his sultry eyes, she thought of warmth. A softer kind of heat than he emitted when hot and sweaty. A cozier heat. Like a blanket. Or a small fire crackling in a hearth. She immediately wanted to cuddle with him.

"Hi," she said, loosening a hand from the baby to open the screen door.

He smiled. "Hi."

And when he stepped inside, the sudden realness of the situation struck Holly all over again. She was about to spend an evening with an attractive man. It was all so strange and unexpected that it took on a surreal quality she could barely comprehend. And it all stemmed from the heat she felt in his presence—every kind—and from that wonderful, horrible readiness. When you truly forget how something feels, you don't expect to ever feel it again, and yet here it was, swallowing her.

"I hope you like steak," she said hopefully.

"Love it," he replied.

"Are you good with a grill?"

He shrugged. "I'm better with a grill than a stove."

"Good enough," she said on a laugh. "Everything's on the patio, if you'd like to go on out."

"You sure there's nothing I can help you carry?" he asked. "I mean, you've kinda got your hands full." He glanced at her baby-filled arms.

"Well," she conceded, "you can get some drinks from the fridge if you want. There's soda, iced tea, and beer. Grab whatever you'd like for yourself, and I'll have some tea."

As he dug in the refrigerator, she freed a hand from Emily and Eeyore to reach for a glass in one of the overhead cabinets.

But Derek quickly rose up. "I can get that for you."

"Thanks," she said softly.

She waited appreciatively as he found a glass and poured her tea. Then he grabbed a beer for himself and carried both drinks out onto the patio, following her.

Taking a seat at the round outdoor table with Emily in her lap, Holly picked up a bottle she'd brought out a few minutes earlier and slid the nipple into Emily's waiting mouth. "If I can get her to drink her bottle and eat her strained peaches while you cook, then we might get to eat an uninterrupted meal," she explained to Derek, who stood with his back to her as he worked at the grill.

"Does that not happen a lot?" he asked over his shoulder. "You getting to eat an uninterrupted meal?"

"Well," she said, thinking it through, "getting interrupted a lot is kind of par for the course with a baby." Then she looked down at Emily and made a silly face. "But she's worth it. Aren't you, sweetie?"

By the time Derek had cooked the steaks and baked potatoes, wrapped in foil, Holly had succeeded in feeding Emily her dinner. She felt a little odd—she'd obviously never been on a date with a baby before, and she hoped Derek didn't find it annoying. But this was the way it had to be. She needed her time with Emily, and Emily needed her mommy time, too.

As she laid Emmy in her carrier and tilted it back into reclining position, she felt guilty about silently willing the baby to fall asleep. But she wanted a little time with this man.

Actually, she wanted a *lot* of time with him.

Still, she'd settle for a little.

To her guilt and joy, Emily did indeed fall asleep, allowing the two of them to share pleasant conversation over dinner—about the weather and the neighborhood and both their jobs. And Holly couldn't deny to herself that it was nice to spend time talking to an adult for a change. She adored being with Emily, of course, and she loved her third graders, as well, but…it was nice to have a real conversation. One that had more depth than the two-minute meetings she had with parents or other teachers.

And nice, too, to have it with such a gorgeous hunk of man. Just sitting next to him, looking into those sexy eyes as they talked, filled her up with something that had definitely been missing. Simple masculinity. Though she'd never thought about it before, it struck her then that sometimes a woman just need to be around that. Life could be full without a man, sure—but there was nothing wrong with enjoying having one around.

"I named the cat," he announced, pushing his empty plate back and lying his used napkin atop it.

Holly smiled. "And the name is?"

"Claws."

She raised her eyebrows. "As in Santa?"

"No," he said, "as in this." Derek then held out his arms, revealing to her that both were covered with deep red scratches from wrist to elbow.

Holly gasped and instinctively reached out to gently touch two fingers to one of the thick red lines.

But she hadn't been thinking, hadn't been expecting the jolt of electricity that coursed through her veins when her fingertips met his skin. Slowly letting her hand come to rest on his arm, she lifted her gaze to his warm, sexy eyes.

Should she offer to kiss the wounds and make them better? Or perhaps she should just offer to rub something on them. Maybe she should forget the scratches altogether and offer to kiss *other* places.

Their eyes locked with an intense heat she'd never quite felt before, and her chest began to tighten. She swallowed, unnerved by the sensations that held them both so still, so on-the-brink of something bigger than she could completely understand. God help her, but she wanted this man. And the look in his eyes was enough to make her think he wanted her, too.

Chapter Four

"WAAA," EMILY POUTED from her carrier.

Oh no. *Not now, Em.* What a time for her to wake up!

And then pouting quickly turned to something louder.

"Waaaaa! Waaaaaaaa!"

With quivering breath, Holly drew both her hand and her gaze away from Derek as her daughter's cries grew more insistent. Emily needed her.

She dropped her eyes to the baby, stooping to swoop her up into her arms. "What's wrong, angel?" she asked, trying to forget the thunderous beating of her heart, trying not to feel the slight trembling of her arms around her child.

"Waaaaaa!"

"Shhhhhh, Emmy," she cooed, standing to rock her. "Shhhh, honey, it's all right."

Derek pushed his hands back through his hair and sighed. Damn it, he knew a baby would interrupt things. His instincts had been right all along. This had been a bad idea from the beginning and he shouldn't have succumbed to his temptation for the pretty schoolteacher.

Still, he knew it wasn't the baby's fault. And, hoping Holly hadn't noticed his reaction, he cautiously glanced up to watch mother and child. Emily's crying had quieted and now Holly began played a game with her, tickling and rubbing the baby's tummy. "Got your belly," she was saying in a silly voice. "Mommy's got your belly."

He supposed most people would find it hard not to think they were cute together. And something about Holly's eyes…as beautiful as they were normally, when she looked at the baby, they seemed to glitter with a new light.

He had to admit it made him a little jealous, even if that was childish—*he'd* like to be the one making those eyes light up so bright. And he had to admit that watching Holly with the baby somehow twisted his stomach, pinched something inside him. It was oddly endearing, and yet it made him uncomfortable. He decided it would be easier to just look away.

"So," she said, suddenly returning her attention to him, "what happened? Why did the cat scratch you?"

"Well, after you figured out how dirty he was this morning, I decided to give him a bath."

And to his surprise, Holly released a pretty trilling laugh, her green eyes going wide. "You *what?*"

"Gave him a bath," he repeated, feeling a little defensive. "What's so funny?"

She tilted her head, a lock of reddish hair falling down over one eye. "Is this your first cat?" she asked knowingly.

Why was he slightly embarrassed about it? "Yes," he admitted.

"Derek," she said, "cats are legendary for not liking water. As in, no one gives their cat a bath."

"Oh," he said. And hell—he felt a little dumb. "Well, my cat lives up to the legend."

She smiled and settled back at the table, Emily in her lap. "So you named him Claws," she said. "That's really cute."

"It is?" He arched one brow.

And when she nodded at him and smiled—damn, his heart did the bending thing again. And he felt wonderful and horrible at the same time. Why did he have to be falling for *this* woman? This woman with her tailored shorts and her crying baby. This woman who was so different from him.

And he was just thinking about leaning over and kissing her—when the phone rang inside the house. *Swell—another interruption.*

"I'll be right back," she said, hoisting the baby onto her hip as she rushed to the back door.

And he nodded, hoping his dismay wasn't as obvious as it felt.

But damn it. He barely knew her, and yet everything she did seemed to excite and entice him. He couldn't believe it, but he'd actually, truly been moved by watching her with the baby a few minutes before. He couldn't understand it and it annoyed him. In fact, even just being here began to annoy him. He didn't want to play daddy to any woman's baby, no matter how alluring she was, so what had he hoped to accomplish by coming here in the first place?

"Derek," she said, her voice suddenly tense as she rushed back out to the patio, "I'm sorry, but I'm going to have to cut the evening short."

He stood up, letting his eyes widen. "What's wrong?"

"My mother is having chest pains of some kind," she said worriedly. "And instead of calling 911, she called me. I need to go over to her house, and I might need to take her to the hospital."

Holly's gaze darted forlornly to the house she'd just exited, her body starting to move first toward the baby carrier, and then back toward the door. Appearing befuddled, she hurriedly shifted the baby from one hip to the other. "I'll need to pack a diaper bag," she mumbled. "And make a bottle. I'd better grab a sweater for you in case it gets chilly. Of all the times for your Aunt Michelle to be out of town on vacation. And—*oh Emily*," she said as the baby spit up all over the pink-ribboned dog on her outfit.

She rushed past Derek to grab a white cloth from the picnic table as he stood there feeling completely useless, then quickly scooped the mess off the dog and wiped the baby's mouth. "I'm sorry, sweetheart," she said. "Mommy's so upset that she's jostling you around and making your dinner come back up."

Shit—how could he help here? He had no idea, but felt compelled to lift some of the load from Holly's pretty shoulders. "What can I do to make this better?" he asked. "Can I drive you? Call someone? Whatever you need."

She stopped, met his gaze with worried eyes. "It's so sweet of you to offer, but there's really nothing. If my sister was in town, I'd call her to watch Emily, but we'll be fine."

"Are you sure?" he asked. Then he looked around the patio, where dirty dishes sat on the table and by the grill. "I can at least clean up the mess after you go."

Her eyes softened just slightly. "Would you? That would be great. One less little thing, you know?"

"I'm happy to," he said. "And it there's anything else…"

She pursed her lips, looking a little overwhelmed, but not answering.

And then Derek heard himself say the most shocking words he'd ever uttered. "I could watch the baby for you."

He barely knew where they'd come from or when he'd turned into such a freaking good Samaritan—but he couldn't help thinking it was one thing she might really need right now.

Even so, her brow knit doubtfully. "That's really sweet, Derek," she said, "but…I don't know if that's really a good idea."

Yeah, he wasn't sure it was a great idea either, but he couldn't help remembering Aunt Marie's last days. And he couldn't stop seeing the worry in Holly's eyes. "Look," he said, "you don't know what you're walking into over there. And like you said, you might have to go to the hospital. Wouldn't it be better to just leave Emily here with me?"

Holly sighed. "This is probably hard for you to understand..." she began, and he helped her out by finishing the thought.

"You're probably thinking that you don't even know me."

"Well..." she replied, her hesitation confirmation enough.

"But I *am* your next door neighbor," he pointed out. "It's not as if you don't know where I live. And I really just want to help you out. You've got enough on your plate right now without having to take care of the baby, too. And besides," he said, leaning down to look at the baby's face, "she seems to be going to sleep anyway. So why not just let her stay here?"

Holly bit her lip, considering his words. She'd never left Emily with anyone she didn't know before. She'd even chosen Miss Carol's daycare because Miss Carol was an old family friend. But everything Derek said made sense to her. Why drag Em out to her mother's, then possibly to the hospital? And how attentive could she be to her baby while she tended to her mother's pains?

She took a deep breath, finally conceding to herself that this would be okay.

"I'm not sure how long I'll be," she warned.

He simply shook his head. "It doesn't matter. It's fine."

"All the important numbers are on the refrigerator," she told him. "My mother's house, Emily's doctor, poison control…"

"Got it," he said.

"And I'll call to let you know what's going on as soon as I can figure it out myself."

Holly still felt apprehensive about the decision, but it would be much easier to see to her mother on her own. And despite the fact that she'd only *officially* met the guy yesterday, she felt like she knew him, at least in a neighborly way. After all, she'd been watching his comings and goings for weeks and the worst behavior she'd seen was the fact that he liked to play his music a little loud. She supposed the most important thing at a time like this was what she felt in her heart, and when she looked there, she saw something in him that inspired her trust.

So she took a deep breath and prepared to hand the sleeping Emily into her neighbor's muscular arms. "Hold her like this, supporting her head," she said, demonstrating.

"I know how to do it," Derek lied, watching her. He wanted to make her feel at ease about leaving the baby.

When she leaned near him, he cradled his arms like hers. And stepping closer, he held his arms beneath the baby, brushing against Holly's stomach during the slow, gentle exchange as her warm arms slid the even warmer baby into his grasp.

She turned then and rushed back toward the house, and upon reaching the door, paused and looked back at him. "Thank you," she said. "Thank you so much."

"You're welcome," he replied.

He listened then as Holly dashed out the front door and started her car. He listened as she backed out and drove away. He listened to the birds still twittering in the trees that lined their backyards. He felt frozen in place. There was a baby in his arms.

He looked down at her and she back up at him. So she was awake, after all. *Well, that's okay—I can handle this.*

Still peering into her eyes, he wondered what the hell she was thinking. He wondered if she would start screaming as soon as she realized her mother was gone. He wondered if she could sense how helpless he felt.

"So...Emily," he said awkwardly, "looks like, uh, it's just me and you for a while."

"Gaaaaa."

And he decided not to say anymore. He still felt weird talking to a baby. Then he remembered that he'd spent the last two days having conversations with a cat. Yep, he was definitely losing his edge.

"Okay," he said to himself, spotting Emily's carrier behind him on the concrete patio, "I'll just set her in here, and then...then we'll go inside." Or...maybe he should try to clean up the dinner mess first. Hell, he didn't know. How closely did she need to be watched? Could she tell he'd never done this before? He had a feeling she could.

He swallowed. How the hell had he managed to volunteer himself for this? What had he been thinking?

But that doesn't matter. You're in it now—deal with it.

And if he was honest with himself, it made him feel good that Holly had entrusted him with what was clearly the most precious thing in her life. It made him want to do a good job for her.

Lowering Emily into the carrier, he turned to the messy table. He gathered the dirty plates and napkins in his arms, but then wondered if he should leave the baby outside while he carried them in. He wasn't sure what he thought might happen to her, yet somehow it didn't seem prudent.

So he sighed and set the dirty stuff back down, then brought Emily inside. Setting the carrier on the dining room table, he went back out and gathered the dinner mess and brought it in to the kitchen.

Then he checked on Emily. What was he supposed to do now? Just stand there and look at her?

He and Emily stared at each other for a few minutes—and then he noticed a pout developing on her face. It was actually sort of cute, but he didn't think it was a good sign.

"Waaa," she said, puckering her brow.

"Geez," he responded, glancing nervously around the

room—for what he didn't know—and then ran one hand back through his hair. "What's wrong?"

"Waaaaaaa," Emily cried much louder. "Waaaaaaaaaa! Waaaaaaa!"

"Oh brother," Derek muttered as the baby broke in to a full scream that he feared could probably be heard in the next state. The neighbors would probably think he was beating her. What the hell should he do?

Then he remembered watching Holly earlier. And he leaned down over the baby and tentatively slid his hands beneath her body to pick her up.

But it didn't work. Still screaming, the baby seemed uncomfortable in his arms as he switched her from one to the other, then turned her around, then cradled her. "Waaaaaaaaaa!"

"I'm sorry," he said above the screaming. "I don't know how to do this. I don't know what you want."

He tried walking around and rocking the baby in his arms, but that did no good, either. Then he spotted the stuffed Eeyore she'd been clutching when he'd come to the door. He snatched it up and held it in front of her face.

"Waaaaaaaa!"

He wiggled the Eeyore back and forth.

"Waaaaa! Waaaaaaaa!"

He kept wiggling Eeyore, mainly because he was out of ideas.

"Waaa…"

And to his wonder and utter astonishment, the crying finally began to subside.

And then, then…Emily even smiled.

But just as quickly she frowned so Derek shook Eeyore once more.

"Aaaaa," she said very calmly, lifting a hand to touch Eeyore's purple ear.

"Do you like Eeyore?" he asked.

"Aaaaa," she said again.

But then her little brow began to crinkle, and her bottom lip pushed back into a pout. "Waaaaaaa!"

He wiggled Eeyore, wiggled him like he'd never wiggled him before—but Eeyore's appeal had apparently waned. "Waaaaaaa! Waaaaaa! Waaaaaaa!"

Aw hell. Derek didn't know what to do. A sweat broke out on his forehead. Maybe something was wrong with the baby. Maybe she was sick. Maybe he should call a doctor. He'd never felt so helpless and inadequate in his life. And he'd felt pretty inadequate before, so that was really saying something.

"Emily, I don't know what's wrong!" he said, exasperated.

And then he smelled something.

He sniffed at the air and—oh boy—it suddenly hit him full force. "Uh-oh," he said, tossing Eeyore aside and then holding the baby out from him with both hands, suspended in mid-air. "*That's* what's wrong with you."

In that particular moment, Derek wished desperately that he had a mother or a sister to call. Aunt Marie sure would have come in handy right now. But he was on his own. And he had promised Holly that he could do this, that he could take care of her baby.

He took a deep breath and tried to block out the noise of the wailing child. *All right—keep a cool head here, Cassidy. Figure this out.*

Still holding her out in front of him, Derek walked around the house until he found the nursery. Decorated in Winnie-the-Pooh from ceiling to floor, it wasn't hard to spot. Going inside made him feel as if he'd just stepped onto foreign ground, into a place he didn't belong. Everything around him seemed too soft, from the Pooh comforter in the baby bed to the pastel colors on the walls. But he couldn't think about that now—he had an angry baby to deal with.

When he spotted a piece of furniture that was padded on top, he figured this must be a place meant for Emily. So he set her down, keeping one hand on her so she wouldn't fall and using the other to snoop in the drawers and compartments beneath her.

Paydirt! He found diapers and wipey things and knew he'd come to the right place.

"Okay," he said, now surveying her poodle-trimmed apparel, "how do we get this thing off you?"

"Waaaaaaaa!"

"You're not much help, you know," he said with a scowl. Then he set about the trying task of undoing buttons and snaps, finally removing Emily completely from the outfit, handling her little limbs like pieces of fine china. She felt fragile and he didn't want to break her.

Next, he located the fasteners on the diaper and undid them. And just when he was beginning to think this wasn't such a hard job after all, he pulled the front of the diaper down.

The contents assaulted his nose and eyes at the same time, forcing him to take a quick step backwards. "Oh my God!" he said. How on earth had she done that?

Taking a minute to regroup, Derek pulled out a large handful of the wipey things. Then took a deep breath and, lifting the baby by her ankles until she was nearly suspended by them, he reached in and wiped, unable to watch what he was doing.

Grabbing more wipes and repeating the ritual several times, he finally decided that the baby was clean enough, or at least as clean as she was going to get, and he moved her naked little body away from the nasty diaper.

Using his fingertips, he lifted the heavy diaper into the garbage can now filled with messy wipes, the sight making him wonder over and over again: *How does anyone stand this?*

Finally—thank God—he got Emily into a fresh, clean diaper. "There," he said.

Then, looking at the poodle suit, which lay in a heap at the corner of the padded table, he decided he'd probably never get it back on her the right way, and he didn't want to do anything that might irritate her again. "Afraid you're gonna have to go topless until your mom gets home," he told her. At least the weather was warm, so he didn't have to worry about her getting cold.

Releasing a huge sigh, Derek reached down and picked up the baby again. He walked to the living room and settled with her on the couch, wrapping one hand around her waist to balance her on his lap. He felt exhausted. And he couldn't believe his date with Holly had ended up like this.

But what a selfish bastard you are. Holly's mother could be in the hospital right now for all he knew, and all he could think about was himself. He was ashamed for being so insensitive, especially after having lost Aunt Marie so recently.

He glanced down at Emily, who sat calmly in his lap. "We're doing okay here, aren't we?" he asked her.

"Gaaaaa," she said.

Well, at least the baby had stopped crying now. She sat placidly looking up at him, her eyes wide and filled with fresh contentment.

And he found himself peering down at her, growing oddly curious when he least expected it.

So on impulse, he reached out to touch the pillowy, pinkish skin of her arm. After which he sat there, a little taken aback, because he'd never felt anything quite so soft or smooth before. *How amazing to know we all started out that way, that soft.*

And that was when Emily rested her hand on top of his.

Leaning his head forward, he gazed down at how tiny her hand was compared to his larger, darker one. And he thought about how delicate her fingers were, especially compared to his, callused and hardened by work.

Instinct made him lift his index finger —and when he did, Emily wrapped her hand around it. And something in his stomach rippled.

HOLLY SWUNG THE car into the driveway, exhausted. One emergency down. Now to relieve Derek of baby duty. He'd probably never want to see her again.

She'd called twice from her mother's house and he'd claimed things were fine—but she could tell he wasn't experienced with babies, so she hurried toward the front door ready to find chaos. She'd been away for almost three hours.

To her surprise, however, she stepped inside a house filled with silence. The lights had been turned low, casting a misty glow across the still living room.

When she spotted them, a soft smile seized her. Derek lay on the couch and Emily had fallen asleep on his chest.

He smiled up at Holly with sleepy eyes, then shifted to a sitting position, careful not to jar the baby with the movement. "How's your mother?" he whispered.

"Fine, I think." She sat down next to them. "It seemed to be a false alarm. The pains went away, but I stayed with her until she fell asleep. She's seeing the doctor tomorrow."

"Good." He nodded.

"So you and Emily did okay?"

"Um, yeah," he said, appearing to think back over their time together. "Pretty bad diaper scene, but we muddled through."

His words made Holly smile—but that was when Derek glanced down at Emmy, his expression changing uncertainly, and he thrust the baby toward her.

She reached out and took her daughter, who stirred only slightly at the movement. "She had a bad one, huh? I'm sorry."

"It's all right," he said. "But I couldn't get her outfit back on her, so…"

"That's fine," she assured him warmly. Then she gazed down at her little girl, feeling awkward about everything that had happened. His sudden change of demeanor as he'd gotten more fully awake had reminded her to. "Do you mind if I put her to bed now?"

He shook his head.

And Holly tried to smile at him, but now the effort proved difficult. What a hell of a way to impress a guy. Invite him to dinner, then make him babysit. "I'll be right back," she told him.

He nodded, still looking sleepy, or maybe disgruntled. She couldn't tell.

Entering the nursery, the smell of the bad diaper attacked her instantly. She rushed Emily into a pink terrycloth sleeper, then lay her gently down in bed, after which she transferred the diaper and used wipes to the Diaper Genie where the rank smell would be swallowed.

Derek had been right—it *was* a nasty diaper.

"'Night, sweetie," she whispered, flipping off the light in Emily's room.

Then she rushed back to the couch and Derek, taking a seat next to him. It surprised her to feel the intense beating of her own heart, but this time, unfortunately, it wasn't due to her attraction to him—now it could only be attributed to her embarrassment at having put him in such a position on what she had originally hoped would qualify as a date.

"I'm so sorry for all this," she began, staring down at her hands in her lap as she spoke. "I feel just horrible. And I can't tell you how much I appreciate you watching Emily for me. And I'm sorry about that awful diaper. I wish you hadn't had to stay with her, but—"

"It's fine," he interrupted her, using his fingertips to lift her chin. The touch had come when she'd least expected it.

And as she looked into his eyes, desire instantly overtook her. Why, oh why, had things had to turn out like this? She only wished…what? She didn't even know. None of her wishes seemed even remotely realistic at the moment. She should have known she had too many other responsibilities in her life right now to have time for a man—even a gorgeous, virile, incredibly sexy one. She hung her head in defeat, whispering, "I'm just sorry the night has to end this way."

When he tilted his head and peered into her eyes, the heat from his nearly made her sweat. "It doesn't have to," he told her.

"It doesn't?" She tried like hell not to be nervous beneath his sultry gaze.

"No," he answered, voice low and sexy. "It could end like this." Then he gently cupped her cheek in his palm and leaned in to give her a small kiss, his lips warm and firm on hers. She felt it all the way to her toes.

"Or it could end like this," he told her—and he kissed her again, longer this time, his mouth opening, his tongue gently sliding between her lips before the kiss ended.

As a weakened sigh left her, her body shuddered with longing and she let him see it in her eyes.

"I can think of more ways for it to end," he told her, a seductive and oh-so-tempting grin reshaping his expression.

And Holly's embarrassment had suddenly faded—turned to something completely different, completely consuming. She felt daring. She felt alive. And she felt...ready. Yes, ready. "What are they?" she asked.

Chapter Five

EREK'S STRONG HAND slid to the back of Holly's neck, drawing her to him. His mouth was more sensual and hungry this time and his tongue more probing. He pushed his way between her lips and she surrendered, letting his tongue capture hers. The idea that their tongues were slow dancing sent a thick wave of pleasure rippling through the small of her back.

When he withdrew, they were both breathless, and his gaze burned through her, conveying a deeper desire than words could describe. The way she felt both frightened and excited her. It had never been like this with Bill. It had never been like this with anyone at all. All the fantasies of her youth seemed suddenly true and real and ready to converge right at this moment.

"I love your hair," he whispered in her ear, nibbling at the lobe, then raining kisses on her neck.

Holly drew in her breath and, for the first time, let herself begin to touch him. Her hands found his chest and she pressed her palms against the muscles hiding beneath his shirt, finding the rapid beat of his heart. It fueled her excitement.

"I want you, Holly," he breathed.

And she wanted him, too—like she'd never wanted a man before. But she could only moan in response.

He lay her gently back on the couch until he was moving atop of her—in a whole different kind of slow dance—their legs intertwining like grapevines. She writhed beneath him, both enraptured at the near-ecstasy that coursed through her body and dumbfounded by how quickly it had happened, how fast she had allowed herself to be caught up in his charms.

His hands found her breasts, kneading them through her clothes as she lay gasping beneath him, wishing she had the strength to tell him to slow down. Because it had just hit her that this was awfully fast. Awfully fast because they'd just met. Awfully fast because this was her very first date since her husband's death.

But she didn't—couldn't. It felt too good. Had *anything* ever felt so good? Had anything ever made her lose control like this before? *Ready.* That word had passed through her mind a little while ago, and she desperately wanted to be that for him. And she'd thought she was— she'd practically felt it coursing through her veins. But was she?

Soon his touches had heightened all her senses and numbed her mind so that she could only *feel*. His thumbs, stroking so delicately over the peaks of her breasts, teasing them into tight buds. His voice, rasping in her ear. "You feel so good. I want to feel more of you."

His hot breath, on her neck—and then drifting, down over the top of her chest, soon warming the hollow between her breasts.

His fingers worked at the buttons of her blouse, first one, then another, then another—as her lips trembled and her heart pounded. She moved beneath him almost involuntarily, her pelvis lifting and rubbing against his, lost in a hundred different delicious sensations. Then his hands were on the lace cups of her bra, squeezing, caressing, making her moan. His fingertips rubbed circles over her nipples and she lifted her eyes to his.

As their gazes locked, he whispered to her. "I want to kiss them."

Oh God. She drew in her breath, longing for what he'd just promised.

Then his tongue thrust between her lips again, hard and hot, but only for a moment before his mouth dropped to her chest, sprinkling tiny licks and kisses— just before his fingers moved to the front clasp of her bra.

The touch was unexpectedly shocking, like reality suddenly reaching out to bite her. *This…isn't me, isn't who I am. This is some irresponsible teenager in the backseat of a car.* Suddenly nothing made sense.

She reached for his hands, stopping their progress, and he looked to her eyes. "What's wrong?" he murmured deeply.

"I can't." She hated the words even as they left her.

"Why not?"

"Because…I hardly know you and we're moving too

fast and this isn't like me and I have a baby sleeping in the next room." The reasons had all suddenly spilled out of her in a rush.

He tilted his head, looking surprisingly undaunted. "We can be quiet," he offered softly. "We won't wake her."

And Lord—the warm timbre of his voice made the invitation tempting. *All* of it was tempting. All of *him*.

But suddenly not tempting enough. "No, that's not it," she explained. "This just doesn't seem…"

"What? It doesn't seem what?"

She bit her lip while the sexy guy on top of her began looking confused and disappointed. She hated the frustration that shone in his eyes. "I'm sorry," she told him. "It's just that…that…"

Holly didn't know what to say. She wanted to tell him that the problem wasn't him, it was her. Her life, her commitments, her responsibilities. She wanted to explain that she'd only had sex with three guys in her life and never on the first date.

Of course, none of those men had ever succeeded in making her feel as completely overcome with desire as she did right now. She felt like the silly, nervous teenager who had dreamed all those wonderful, crazy dreams of perfect passion without ever letting any of them find her, without ever letting any of them come true. And then when they finally did, she pushed them away. In fact, she felt positively pre-adolescent.

And feeling so childish was horrible enough without

letting him in on it, too.

"Waaaaaaaaa! Waaaaaa! Waaaaaaaaa!"

The baby's cries, cutting into his frustration and her inability to explain, just seemed like the cherry on top of the sundae of awkwardness, and a perfect reminder of why this couldn't happen. And also, at the moment, a good reason to escape having to explain.

"I have to get her," Holly said, slipping desperately out from beneath him.

She buttoned her blouse as she ran to the nursery, then scooped Emily up in her arms.

"Oh Emmy," she cooed, rocking the baby to calm her, then cuddling her daughter to her chest. "What's wrong, sweetheart? Mommy's sorry she was gone all night. But I'm here now. Mommy's here."

She kissed Emily on the forehead and tried to reconcile the wholesome love she had for her child with the reckless abandon she'd been swimming in just moments before. She wasn't sure the two could co-exist peacefully.

And it was tempting to consider just staying where she was, in the nursery, soft and comforting by its very design—and right now a safe place because she and Emily were alone here, not having to face the uncomfortable situation she'd let develop.

Too bad she couldn't just stay here all night. *But you have to go back out there. You have to stop* acting *like a silly, embarrassed teenager, even if you still feel like one.*

Gathering her courage, she carried Emily out into the living room. Derek was standing up now, but his T-shirt remained untucked and his rumpled hair made him look a little dangerous. The very sight of him re-immersed her in her fantasies.

"Derek, I'm sorry," she told him.

But he held up a hand to stop her. "Don't apologize. I was pushy."

"No," she said. "You weren't." And she meant it. She'd given him every indication that she wanted more of him. And she *had* wanted more of him. She just hadn't been able to go through with it. She hadn't been as ready as she'd thought.

"Listen," he said, "it's late."

She simply nodded. Even though he hadn't thought it was late a few minutes ago.

"I should go," he told her.

"All right," she said, more meekly than intended.

"Good night," he said. And then he turned to leave.

"Derek," she said quickly, stopping him. She couldn't let him leave this way—she had to somehow try and repair what she'd messed up.

And when he turned to face her again, she said, "I'm…really sorry."

He shook his head. "It's okay. There's nothing to be sorry for. And…thanks for dinner. Dinner was nice."

Dinner was *nice. Only too short.* Like the things they both were saying right now. There was so much they *weren't* saying. Or…maybe none of it mattered and that was why neither of them were bothering to say it. The tone of their talk now, a certain shortness to it, suggested a certain finality.

"Thank *you* for watching Emily," she replied. Still just as short. Still not one of the things she thought she should be saying here.

He only nodded, and then walked out the door—and she watched him go. She *let* him go.

And then she carried Emily to the couch, where she sat down and cried.

DEREK WALKED THE distance from Holly's house to his without feeling the ground beneath his feet, without being aware of the darkness, or the stars in the sky, or the cool summer breeze that floated through the night air. He felt like a balloon that had been deflated.

Stepping inside, he turned on the light to see a fluffy white kitten perched on the arm of his couch. He walked over and scratched the blue-eyed cat behind the ears. "You clean up pretty good," he said, still a little amazed to discover his cat was white.

He continued to pet the kitten as he took a seat on the couch next to him, and Claws purred and nuzzled against Derek's hand. He figured that must mean the cat had gotten over their little bath disagreement earlier. He pulled him into his lap, surprised at the urge to hold him.

Maybe it wouldn't be so bad to be a cat guy, after all.

Still, being a cat guy did not a romance make. Because being a cat guy did not equate to being a baby guy.

He and Emily had survived tonight, and that was about it.

Besides, he was beginning to think his original instincts had been correct. Holly wasn't ready for dating yet.

Not that there was anything wrong with not wanting to go to bed on the first night—he could have lived with that, respected her wishes on it. But he had seen too much apprehension in her eyes. Her worries, fears—whatever they were—had to do with more than knowing each other for a proper length of time before having sex. And he'd thought perhaps she was about to tell him what those fears and worries were when the baby had started crying and blown any chance they'd had of making the night a success. Derek shook his head, frustrated by the whole situation.

"I don't think I'm going to see her again," he said, thinking out loud.

Claws looked up at him and they made eye contact. "Meow."

So Derek sighed and told the cat, "It's just best that way." After all, there were too many things that would make a relationship between them too hard, too many things to keep them apart.

They had nothing in common—that was clear.

And the further truth was that she really had no idea just exactly how much in common they *didn't* have.

Some of the differences between them were easy to see, right there on the surface. She had a baby, and he was just learning to function with a cat. She was soft and pretty, and he was hard and dirty.

But some of the differences went deeper. Too deep.

Holly had probably been brought up in a nice middle-class neighborhood like this one. She'd probably lived in a nice home and slept in a bed with frills and a canopy. She'd probably gone shopping for school clothes every fall. Hell, she'd probably been a cheerleader. Or the editor of the school newspaper. Or in some other important position.

Her conservative little soul would probably be shocked beyond repair to find out what *his* childhood had been like. Some days he was lucky enough to forget about it—he'd come a long way and he'd put it behind him. But that didn't change the facts. It didn't erase the things he'd been through. No matter how far away he traveled from his youth, it would always be there, a part of him, a part of his history.

Besides, he told himself, shifting his thoughts back to Holly, babies plus conservatism did not equal the kind of relationship he generally looked for. It was a shame that the woman of his dreams had to come with those particular features.

Wait a minute. *Woman of his dreams?* Was that what Holly Blake was?

If someone had asked him to describe his dream woman a couple of days ago, he wouldn't have made her a schoolteacher. And he wouldn't have dressed her in ridiculously high-necked clothing and nightgowns like

Aunt Marie had worn. And, of course, then came the obvious: a picture of his dream woman would not have included a baby.

And yet Holly had all those things and still managed to twist his mind into contemplating the idea that she might just possibly be the woman he'd been waiting for his whole life.

Even though, before this moment, it had never occurred to him that he might be waiting for someone. It was a hard thing to understand.

"Meow," Claws said, climbing up his chest to nuzzle at his throat. He wrapped one hand around the cat's back.

"And now, because of her," Derek said, "I have a cat." He looked down at Claws, then shook his head. "Lost the girl, got the cat. Figures."

"Meow," Claws protested.

"I guess you're really not so bad," he admitted, pulling back to look down his nose at the miniature cat. Then he shrugged. "In fact, I kinda like you in white."

Realizing that it was past midnight, he detached the cat from his chest, lowered him to the floor, and went into his bedroom. Stripping down to his underwear, he pulled back the covers, then lay down, hoping for fast sleep. He didn't want to think about Holly Blake anymore. He didn't want to think about anything.

He almost wished Aunt Marie was here to talk to, but he quickly stopped the impossible thought—it was useless to wish for what you could never have. He had to face it—he was alone now and he had to get used to it. No wonder he was talking to cats.

DEREK LAY ON the old, nubby couch watching TV. Scooby Doo. His favorite. The picture on the screen was fuzzy and sometimes it rolled, but that was okay.

His father was sleeping. He slept late on Saturday mornings.

Actually, his father slept late every morning, but weekends were the only time Derek could enjoy it—the other days he had to get himself up and off to school.

The scent of alcohol hung in the house, in the room. It seemed to seep from the furniture, from the floor, from the peeling wallpaper all around him. How could one man fill a whole house with the way he smelled?

Then footsteps. Angry footsteps. Too quick for Derek to think or move. A familiar and helpless dread converged on him and he froze in place. His chest went hollow, empty.

"What the hell ya think you're doin'? Get your lazy ass off that couch and get me somethin' to eat!" The voice came slurred, hard to understand as the stench of alcohol on his father's breath gushed down over him, stale and potent.

Derek stared at his father for a second, wishing vaguely for some kind of escape, then started to rise from the couch.

"You deaf, boy?"

He hadn't moved fast enough, and a still-heavier odor of alcohol pressed down on him as the first thrashes came. His curled into a ball on the couch—not a decision but a physical reaction, like those little gray pill bugs that curled into a circle when you tried to kill them—and-instinctively used his arms to cover his head. He gritted his teeth and fought back tears, but stayed as quiet as possible. Talking back only made it worse, made it last longer. Stay quiet and eventually he just got bored with it.

Derek's eyes jolted open and found the blank whiteness of the ceiling. Sweat drenched his body—the sheets stuck to him.

Looking around, he recognized his bedroom. Recognized his life.

It's over, not really happening.

I'm thirty-one years old, not a kid anymore.

I'm in a different world now where everything's okay

He sighed with a mixture of sadness and relief.

"Meow."

"And I have a cat," he said, lifting his head to glance in the direction of Claws' voice. The white kitten perched on his stomach.

He reached up to pet Claws, at the same time lying back to stare again at the ceiling. Damn, it had been a long time since he'd had any of those dreams. But every now and then, one snuck up on him, reminded him. It still had the ability to shake him. And to take him back there.

He took a deep breath, then checked the clock beside his bed. His alarm would go off in five minutes anyway, and he didn't particularly feel like lying there rehashing the dream, or the reality behind it. Lifting Claws off his stomach, he pushed back the covers and trudged to the shower.

Maybe this was Holly's fault. If he hadn't been thinking about how different they were, he probably wouldn't have invited those memories to start skulking around in his subconscious. He turned on the water and let it blast down over him and bring him that much more back to reality.

As he showered, he realized that he was actually looking forward to going to work today, looking forward to toiling away in the hot sun. Hard work was good for the soul, Aunt Marie had always told him. And it was also good for occupying your mind.

Out there on the job site, with hammers and nails and two-by-fours, that was where he belonged. Unlike in Holly Blake's house, or even in her life. He wished he'd never let that pretty face lure him over to help her with her windshield wiper fluid. He wished he'd never laid eyes on her at all.

Quit thinking about her, for God's sake. Just go to work and have a nice, normal day. And maybe afterward he would pick up those flowers and take them to the cemetery like he'd meant to a couple days ago.

Ten minutes later, he poured Claws some milk and opened the last can of tuna in his cabinets. He'd have to stop and pick up some cat food on the way home, too. "See ya, Claws," he said as he left.

He'd almost made it to his truck when he saw Holly step out onto her front porch. Damn. He quickened his pace. With her once again toting Emily on her hip, it was like a flashback to yesterday morning, except that today she wore a thin, cotton gown, white with a blue flower print—no robe—and he thought if he looked hard enough, he might be able to see through it. And except that today he wanted, as much as possible, to avoid her.

"Good morning," she said, stooping to get her paper.

He took a deep breath, then lifted his eyes to her. He tried not to see her beautifully messy hair, or the smile that had the ability to entrance him. "Morning," he replied, reaching to open the door of his pickup.

"How's Claws?" she asked.

"Better, now that he's cleaned up," he replied. Then he swung his gaze in her direction. "Oh, I forgot to tell you, you were right. He's white." Damn it, though. He hadn't exactly meant to make conversation with her—it had just popped out. Why did he have to find her so easy to talk to?

"Want to come in for some coffee?" she asked. Her voice sounded tentative, hopeful.

Which made it harder to turn her down.

But he did anyway. "Um, no thanks—can't. Running late," he said. Even though it was exactly the same time that he'd bumped into her yesterday morning.

"Oh," she said, sounding a little crestfallen but also clearly trying to cover it. "Okay."

"See ya," he said, hopping quickly into the truck and slamming the door.

And he didn't know if she answered because he reached down and twisted the volume knob on the radio, turning it up loud, appreciating loud music more than ever, this morning of all mornings, because it might help drown out all the stuff inside him he didn't want to pay attention to.

Chapter Six

HOLLY SAT ON a wooden stool at the head of the classroom. One by one, she read the words on the spelling test out loud to her class.

"Traveling."

But her mind wasn't on the spelling test. In fact, it wasn't even anywhere in the school building. It was back at her house, in her living room, last night, in the arms of Derek Cassidy.

What a fool she'd been! First leading him on, and then not even taking the time to explain. She'd been so frightened of her own emotions that she'd just wanted to be close to Emily, to hold her, to feel safe. Derek, of course, had just the opposite effect on her. Beneath the weight of his passionate kisses, Holly had felt completely reckless, completely out of control.

"Suitcase."

But was that so bad? Was it so horrible to feel a little bit reckless for once in her quiet life?

Okay, that's it. I have to quit being so uptight, quit being so concerned with what's proper. Just because a woman became a mother didn't mean she lost all feelings of desire.

And if the past few days were any indication, maybe becoming a mother somehow actually *increased* it.

She glanced back down at the spelling list and found her place. "Here's a tricky one," she told the class. "Vacation."

She watched the puzzled looks on their little faces, and inside she smiled knowingly. How much simpler it would be if she were only stumped over the words on a spelling test, rather than stumped over her entire life.

PULLING IN THE parking lot at the daycare center, Holly slid the gearshift into Park, then rushed into the small brick building. Her eyes fell immediately on Emily.

The baby beds here were different than Emily's friendly Pooh-adorned bed at home—here the wooden slats somehow reminded Holly of prison cells. It was no fault of Miss Carol's, but she just hated leaving her baby for eight hours each day.

"Hey, sweetie," she said, giving Emily a big smile as she approached the bed that held her daughter and reached inside to pick her up. She cuddled the child to her chest, then pulled back to kiss her soft little forehead.

Emily returned her smile, accompanied with slobbering, and Holly grabbed a burping cloth from the diaper bag next to the bed to wipe her daughter's mouth. "You're Mommy's good girl," Holly said.

Gathering Emily's belongings, she waved across the room to Miss Carol on her way out the door. Most days she stopped to chat with the caretaker for a few minutes, just to find out how Emily's day had gone, but today she was in a bit of a hurry.

Instead of putting Emily in the car, though, Holly made the split-second decision to venture into the play yard outside the daycare facility. True, she was in a hurry, but she already felt guilty about what she'd decided to do tonight, especially after having been away for so long the previous evening, so she resolved to at least make a little time for her daughter right *now*.

She moved through the grass toward a big concrete turtle that sat near the swings and slides where the older children played. Lowering the diaper bag onto the turtle's shell and Emily's carrier to the ground, she dug out a small quilt and spread it in the grass. Then she lay Emily on the quilt, sitting down beside her.

"Got your belly," she said, ticking the baby through her sleeper. And Emily giggled—*got your belly* was one of her favorite games. But even as Holly continued to make her daughter smile and release small spurts of laughter, her mind drifted.

When she'd come home from the hospital last night, Derek and Emily had looked completely cozy together. She almost even had the impression that they'd bonded a little or something. She didn't think she'd ever seen anything so adorable in her life and just remembering it warmed her heart.

And so, despite herself, she was trying to think of a plan, of some way to show Derek that she really *did* want something with him and that she really *could* make time for him in her life. If she got another chance, she wanted to do things differently—not screw it up like she had last night.

And that was why she was in a hurry, not to mention why she was starting to feel incredibly guilty—for wanting to spend her time away from work in any way that didn't involve Em.

She gazed down to find Emily peering expectantly into her eyes. "Honey," she said, "you're going to be spending the night at Aunt Michelle's house tonight."

"Waouuu."

Holly wasn't trying to get rid of her daughter. Really, she wasn't. But she had to face it—life went on after motherhood. And there were times when mother and baby needed to be apart, even if it was very hard. "Aunt Michelle is always saying how she never gets to see enough of you," she said to help reassure herself. "And you know how you love going over there. Your cousin, Nicholas, has that bright mobile you like so much—remember? It always makes you smile."

"Gaaaa."

Still, despite her own words, the guilt continued to eat at Holly. After all, how could she leave Emmy after waiting all day just to be with her? How could she choose anything over their precious mother-daughter time?

And then that other part of her—that alive, *ready*

part that she'd encountered so often since meeting Derek a couple days ago—whispered in her ear when she'd least expected it. *Aren't mommies entitled to just a little fun? A little romance?*

She released the breath she didn't even realize she'd been holding. That voice was the little push she needed to go through with this.

"Tomorrow's Friday," she told Emily, "and after that we'll have the whole weekend together. I promise. So," she said, "do you mind giving Mommy the night off?"

"Aaaaa," Emily said, this time smiling boldly up at her with twinkling eyes and a bit of spittle at the corners of her mouth. Then a bird twittered in the distance and Emmy pointed a tiny finger toward the noise, making Holly smile.

HOLLY HAD CALLED her sister, Michelle, from school at lunchtime, knowing that her family had returned from their Florida vacation sometime this morning. She hated to impose on her sister this soon after coming home, but she also knew Michelle didn't mind. Michelle had a ten-month-old son of her own, and had told Holly not to even bother going home for supplies—Nicholas had some unisex clothing and would be willing to share with his cousin.

Michelle had sounded thrilled to hear her actually wanting to spend an evening on her own, and she supposed her sister's excitement over the occasion was warranted. Holly had been completely wrapped up in Emily since the day she was born, maybe even more so than most new moms—considering Bill's death.

Though it had been difficult to have just picked Emily up and to already be dropping her off again. And she'd been in the process of saying a prolonged goodbye when Michelle had grabbed her shoulders and herded her toward the door. "She'll be fine, Mommy," her sister insisted.

"Call if she needs me for anything—"

"*She'll be fine, Mommy,*" Michelle said again, this time more emphatically. Then she gently shoved Holly outside.

Holly had stood on the porch, peering in as her sister grabbed up one of Nicholas' stuffed toys and wiggled it merrily before Emmy's eyes. Emmy's smile, as usual, warmed Holly's heart, and finally made her feel it was all right to leave.

Now, driving home, she appreciated her older sister's gruffness. If not for Michelle's insistence, she might have changed her mind and brought Emily home like usual.

And she supposed she shouldn't think about Emily anymore if she could help it. Of course, it would be impossible to block her baby out of her mind entirely, but she had taken Emily to Michelle's for a reason, and she figured she'd better start thinking about that reason, or more precisely, thinking of a plan.

When Holly pulled into the driveway, Derek's truck was still gone—he wasn't home from work yet. But he'd be there soon—even before she'd met him, the music he blasted through the neighborhood had let her grow accustomed to his afternoon schedule.

When she stepped inside the house, she felt funny at first to be there without Emily.

But don't think about Emily. Think about Derek. Think about last night. Think about all the things he could have done to you if you hadn't panicked and run away from him.

So she shut the door to Emily's nursery, hoping that having it out of sight would help keep Emily out of mind, as well. Then she sat down on the couch and tried to think.

She *could* just be honest. She could pick up the phone and call him, explaining very gracefully that she'd been foolish last night and that she hoped he'd allow her to make it up to him.

But no. She'd acted so frightened and awkward that she'd have to do something a little more convincing if she wanted him to give her another chance.

On a lark, she rushed to her bedroom and began digging in her underwear drawer. At the bottom, she found what she sought—black lace lingerie she'd gotten at her wedding shower three years ago. Michelle had given it to her, but she'd never worn it—she'd never had the inclination somehow, never thought of herself as the kind of woman who could get away with that kind of blatant sexiness.

She had a feeling Michelle would approve if she wore

it tonight.

But then what? She let out a forlorn sigh. Was she going to go knock on his door and dance around his living room in it? Do some kind of strip tease? Nope, besides how silly the idea sounded, she'd never have the guts to just show up on his doorstep wearing it anyway.

Think of something that's more you.

Leaving the bedroom, she wandered aimlessly around the house, hoping for inspiration. And once in the kitchen, she glanced out the window, slightly dismayed to see that he still wasn't home. She checked her watch—he was late.

Then she glanced around her. It was a perfectly organized, everything-in-its-place room. She had more spatulas and ladles and spoons than she could put to good use because she had an affinity for kitchen gadgets and seemed to accumulate them by the dozens.

Then an idea hit her. She could cook for him. They said food was the way to a man's heart, and it just so happened that she was a pretty good cook. Though she hadn't made many big meals since Bill had died, because it was difficult to cook for one. So maybe she'd find some way to sneak into his house, set his table, start a fabulous dinner, and surprise him when he finally got home.

But wait—bad idea. Sneaking into his house? That was more than a little intrusive. He'd have every right to be angry. And it might create an even much more awkward situation than the one she was trying to make up for.

And besides, what if he didn't come home at all?

He was *always* home by now.

So what if he had some hot date tonight and had gone to her place to change? Or what if he just went to her place, period?

She tried in vain to recall if Derek had been carrying anything besides his lunchbox this morning, like a change of clothes. And she decided she would actually prefer that to the alternative—because the idea of some chick rolling around with him while he was still hot and sweaty and dirty from work made her feel completely sick with jealousy!

She tried to imagine the kind of woman Derek might be seeing. Probably someone who wore too much makeup.

And skirts that were way too short.

Tramp.

Of course, a woman like that probably wasn't afraid to wear sexy lingerie. In fact, she probably had dozens of sexy bras and panties and nighties in every shape, color, and revealing fabric known to man, and she was probably putting on a fashion show for Derek right this very minute.

Utterly dejected, Holly released a huge sigh and checked her watch. The fashion show would probably end soon and then the two of them would probably start making out on *her* couch. And *she* probably wasn't acting like a scared fifteen-year-old, running to the next room to hide.

That's it—it's hopeless. And over. I blew it and it's too late to fix it.

"Damn it!" she groused. Then she kicked the wall, and watched as the shelf above the phone came tumbling down, neatly spilling all her cookbooks into the kitchen garbage can.

And from outside, she heard a blast of loud music that grew nearer and nearer until finally it stilled—right next door.

He was home.

And she had a broken shelf.

Perfect!

DEREK TRIED NOT to even glance at Holly's house. He'd somehow ended up feeling guilty for turning her down so abruptly this morning. And she'd stayed on his mind all damn day.

He'd thought about last night. He'd thought about her soft lips melding against his, her delicate tongue rolling in sensuous circles inside his mouth. He'd thought about her breasts, so firm and plump in his hands, her nipples taut and inviting. He wished he'd gotten to kiss them.

But he wasn't going to think about her anymore. And he wasn't going to see her again. No matter how much his heart wanted him to.

He'd gone to the cemetery after work and taken a

nice late summer bouquet for the vase on Aunt Marie's headstone. He didn't believe in standing around talking to graves, but he'd stayed for a little while and somehow felt the way she always *used* to make him feel—a little less alone in the world.

Then he'd stopped at the grocery store and picked up some milk and a five-pound bag of food for Claws. He'd found some that said it was especially for kittens.

Exiting the truck with his milk and cat food, he headed inside.

HOLLY WAITED. TEN minutes. Fifteen. Twenty. She didn't want to look like she'd been spying on him out the window, calling as soon as he got home. Though remembering the bag of cat food he'd toted under his arm brought a soft smile to her face.

Then she decided to wait even longer, so she made a sandwich. Then she ate it.

Then she decided to change clothes, which was tricky. What should she wear? Everything she owned looked so much like...well, like it belonged to a school-teacher. She wanted him to forget that boring, pristine side of her and see someone new. But she also didn't want to look like she was trying too hard.

She finally decided on a pair of faded jeans and a white sleeveless summer blouse. For a twist, she tied the blouse in a knot at the waist. It looked casual, like she was just cleaning the house or something. But it also showed just a tiny bit of tummy.

Forty-two minutes after Derek had come home, she finally picked up the phone. Of course, by then she was nervous. She felt like she was calling to invite him to the prom. "Grow up," she whispered to herself. *That's exactly what I'm trying to do here.*

Holding the slightly soiled business card he'd given her when they'd met, she ran her finger over the raised letters that spelled out *Derek*. How girlish it felt to derive joy just from touching his name that way. Silly, but this time in a better way.

Gathering her courage, she dialed the number on the card. And trembled as she tried to breathe. "Relax," she instructed herself as she listened to first one ring, then two.

He picked up on the third. "Hello."

"Derek? This is Holly."

"Oh."

Well, okay then. She suddenly remembered why she'd always hated talking to boys on the phone—it was so difficult to gauge reactions when you couldn't see someone's face. Was that a pleased *oh* or a disappointed *oh*?

She took a deep breath and went on. "I hope I didn't catch you at a bad time."

"No. Just watching some TV."

"Well," she hesitated, "the reason I'm calling is…my shelf fell down."

"Your shelf fell down," he repeated. She was starting

to feel stupid.

"And so...I was wondering if you might be able to help me put it back up...sometime."

On the other end of the line, he hesitated, and Holly's stomach started to hurt. This had been a mistake.

Finally, he said, "Well, how about...now?"

Okay, maybe *not* a mistake. Maybe. "Sure," she said, trying to sound very easy-going about it all as her body betrayed her with an explosion of tiny all-over tingles. "Now's...good."

"Let me grab my toolbox," he said, "and I'll be over in a minute."

Holly hung up the phone nearly in a state of panic. She hadn't even been this nervous last night when he'd been kissing her and touching her and kneading her breasts. It felt different now, because last night had evolved naturally, unexpectedly—and tonight, she was inviting him over with the definite intent to seduce.

Then it hit her. *I'm planning to seduce a man!*

Was she crazy? What made her think she could pull off such a thing?

And especially with *that* man—a man who seemed very capable of seduction on his own. He'd clearly been around the block, and she, by comparison, seemed afraid to even leave her own yard.

But it was too late to back out now. And besides, she'd been upset all night and all day about having ruined things with him, so she must really like the guy. And must really want the guy, too.

"Be a grown-up," she told herself one last time. Then the doorbell rang.

DEREK STOOD ON Holly's front porch, waiting.

His heart had flip-flopped when he'd answered the phone and found her on the other end. He couldn't help feeling relieved to hear she'd only called about a broken shelf. And at the same time, he also couldn't help being disappointed that that was all she wanted.

Not that he had any interest in resuming their very brief relationship. He didn't. But on the other hand, it was hard to consider Claws very good company when he knew Holly was right next door being gorgeous.

"I can do this," he told himself. "I can have a nice, neighborly, platonic relationship with her."

"Hi," she said, smiling as she opened the door to let him inside.

Geez, he prayed she hadn't heard him talking to himself.

And since when did he talk to himself?

Since meeting *her*.

"Hi," he replied. Stepping into the living room, he tried very hard not to look at her. He tried not to see her flowing hair. Or her sparkling green eyes. Or the delectable hint of white tummy between her blouse and her blue jeans. God, she looked good in blue jeans.

"Thanks for coming over," she said. "It's in here, in the kitchen."

She led and he followed.

"Darn thing just fell off the wall a little while ago."

Derek surveyed the situation. "This shouldn't take long to fix," he told her.

And Holly surveyed *him*. He wore khaki cargo shorts and a plain T-shirt like the ones he wore to work. The shirt afforded Holly a delicious view of the sinewy muscles in his arms and chest, and when he turned his back to work on the shelf, she experienced the odd and very unexpected urge to reach out and knead the corded flesh of his shoulders. She watched the hard muscles shift beneath his skin as he worked, the heat in her body beginning to rise. How had she ever managed to push him away last night?

"Doesn't look like the bracket was nailed into a stud," he told her.

"Oh," she breathed.

What had he just said? She was too busy watching his muscles. Something about a stud?

"To find the stud," he explained, "you do this." Then he used his fist to knock lightly on the drywall until the sound changed from a hollow one to a solid one. "See the difference?" he said, knocking again on the hollow area, then the solid.

"Uh huh," she said, vaguely wondering what a stud was, besides a man like him, a man who was arousing the hell out of her by simply examining a wall.

She watched then as he attached the bracket to the wall. "But instead of using nails," he explained, "I'm going to use screws."

"Screws," she repeated dumbly. Then she watched the muscles in his shoulders and arms moving some more as he twisted the screw into the wall. It looked like he was exerting himself and she liked it. Although she could suddenly think of better ways for him to do that. And she was sorry when the screws were in place and the muscles stilled. She wanted to watch him work some more.

"What now?" she asked.

"Well, now," he said, "I'm done." He reached for the fallen shelf and easily rested it on the two brackets that jutted from the drywall.

And disappointment flooded Holly's body.

"I guess I'll see you later," he told her when she didn't reply in any way, dropping his tools back in the small toolbox he'd brought with him.

And then the disappointment that pumped through her veins was replaced with desperation. She hadn't gone through all this just to let him leave.

She'd imagined the job would take longer, that they would chat more, make small talk, that she'd offer him a drink. And she certainly hadn't let her entire body get into the act of watching the man twist screws into studs only to let him walk away that easily.

So she knew she had to do something, and she knew she had to do it now.

"I want you," she blurted.

Chapter Seven

D EREK'S HEAD DARTED around until he faced her with wide eyes. "You what?"

Despite the fact that she couldn't believe what she'd just said, she knew she had no other choice but to plow full steam ahead now.

"I said I want you."

He squinted slightly. "You want me?" And he sounded puzzled, like he didn't understand the words.

Okay—a little surprise had been one thing, but she hadn't counted on outright confusion. She took a deep breath and decided the only thing to do at this juncture was to spill her guts and make her intentions completely clear, come what may.

"I want to rip your clothes off and make love to you right here and now," she told him. She could hear her own heartbeat. And she knew her voice had trembled, but she didn't care. She didn't look down, she didn't cower, she met his gaze head on.

And when he didn't respond, the wonderful and surprising power of being able to shock him pulsed through her entire being—and she followed the startling urge to continue, to tell him just exactly what was on her mind. "I was crazy to let you leave last night. I spent all night and all day today wanting you to touch me. And kiss me. Everywhere."

His eyes glazed then, turning sexy on her. And she got the feeling he was finally beginning to believe her.

But something made her continue anyway. "And watching you now, watching you work, all I want to do is feel you, all over."

After that, though, she finally shut up. Then bit her lip and waited.

She'd completely and shamelessly bared her soul. The rest was up to him. Her heart felt like it might leap from her chest, yet other parts of her were so aroused that her fear hardly mattered. Her desire surpassed her doubts completely.

Derek glanced around them, then returned his heat-filled eyes back to her face. "One question," he said, his voice low and raspy. "Where's the baby?"

"Gone," she answered succinctly. "Spending the night with my sister."

Again, he squinted slightly. "Why?"

And, hell, she'd told him everything else—why not just be honest about this, too? "So I could seduce you without interruption."

He studied her for a moment more, his smoldering gaze nearly burning a hole in her body, and then his eyes took on a wickedly playful glow. "I don't think I've ever been seduced quite so quickly."

"I was nervous," she admitted. "I couldn't go slow."

His breath came harder now as he continued to devour her with his eyes. "I don't think I can, either."

And with that, he took a step toward her, reached for her hands, and gently held them in place on each side of her. Then he stepped in close, grazing the front of her body with his. She sighed at the flutter of pleasure that rippled through her. *Oh God, this is really going to happen!*

Fingers interlocked, her hands imprisoned by his, he pressed firmly into her, pushing her back against the refrigerator. And she heard her own labored breath as she looked up into his eyes.

His lips came down hard on hers, his tongue invading her mouth as his hands slid to her hips, then around to cup her bottom. She kissed him back voraciously, her body succumbing to a whirlwind of sensations, each too quick and powerful for her to assess.

She wrapped her arms about his neck and they kissed again and again as he spun her around, then lifted her up onto the kitchen counter. She spread her legs and let him stand between them, the pressure of his crotch against hers causing a groan to escape from her throat.

"Mmm, honey," he breathed, kissing her neck.

She lifted her arms above her head, clutching helplessly at the wooden cabinets behind her and melting in a hundred different ecstasies, each one vibrant and new.

"So hot," he murmured, now pushing her breasts

together and lowering frantic kisses through her blouse.

She wrapped her legs around his hips and felt him thrusting against her, felt the pulsing that started at the crux of her thighs and spread outward until it reached the tips of her fingers and toes. "Oh, Derek," she breathed. "Derek."

Panting, labored breaths left her as he ripped at the knot in her shirt, then worked hurriedly at her buttons before shoving the blouse away and reaching for the front clasp of her bra.

"Oh...." she sighed when her breasts were freed— and then came his hands and his lips, molding and licking and sucking as she wrapped her legs tighter and tighter, pulling him against her below, again and again. She clutched at his shoulders, ran her fingers through his hair, felt as if she were someone else—and then basked in the marvelous pleasure and knowledge that, no, she was still herself, Holly Blake, and that this man was making her feel things she'd never even known existed, that this man wanted her as badly as she wanted him, that this man was making her moan.

"Please," she rasped without quite meaning to.

He pulled back from her breasts and gazed up at her, his eyes filled with hunger. "Please what, honey?"

She didn't even know. But then she did. "Everything. Just...everything."

He pushed her blouse and bra off her shoulders and she shrugged free of them, then reached for his T-shirt, sliding her hands beneath. Then he ripped the shirt off over his head and her eyes fell on his strong, beautiful chest. "I want to rub against it." More unintended words.

"Go ahead," he said throatily.

And without hesitation, Holly unlocked her legs from his waist and hopped down from the counter—and this time *she* backed *him* into the refrigerator. She raked the tips of her breasts against his chest and they both released low moans that heated the air around them.

She wasn't sure if he reached for her zipper first, or if she reached for his—but they soon tugged at each other's pants, pulling at waistbands, trying to get to each other. They dropped to their knees, kissing frantically, and Holly gave up on Derek's shorts and ran her hands over the muscles she'd admired earlier—in his arms, his shoulders, his chest.

Lying on the kitchen floor, he removed her jeans and her panties—she wriggled out of them as he pulled. And her lips trembled as she watched him finish undressing, whispering, "Hurry." She didn't think she could stand to wait another moment before having him inside her. This was really happening and a freight train couldn't stop it now.

When they were both finally naked, she reached for him. "Now."

"Wait," he breathed.

"*What?*"

Frustrated by the delay, she waited as he reached for the shorts he'd just discarded, then dug in the pocket for his wallet.

"What are you…?" But then she saw the small foil packet and said, "Oh." She might have felt stupid if her arousal hadn't overridden it.

She watched him put it on, biting her lower lip.

And when he was done, he lifted his eyes to hers and caught her staring. "What?" he asked.

"I…like the way you look down there," she confessed in a whisper.

"Oh God," he breathed in low reply—and then he dove on her, pressing her flat against the ceramic tile. She closed her eyes as he used his hands to part her legs. "Are you ready?" he asked.

Ready. That word again. She'd wanted to be that for him last night and couldn't. Tonight, though, she was. She really was.

"I'm more ready than you can imagine," she promised.

And then he was inside her, filling her with himself, filling that part of her that had felt so empty for so long now. He was moving on her, in her, making her cry out as he murmured words of passion over her. "So good, baby—so good."

She listened to his labored breath and relished the way their excitement mixed and mingled, the way their bodies moved so incredibly well together.

"Oh…" She breathed, soaking in the pure joy of it, the connection of it, feeling consumed by it.

She opened her eyes and found his sultry gaze once

again, penetrating her in *that* way nearly as much as he was below. His breathing grew more audible and intense with his thrusts, and Holly lifted herself against each. "Unh..." she moaned.

"Aw God, Holly," he whispered. "God...yeah."

She met each drive of his hard body with as much force as she could, wanting to feel him still more, deeper, deepest. She'd wondered if it would feel strange to be this intimate with a man she didn't know very well, but now that she was, she realized that touching him—and being touched by him—was easy, and that having him inside her felt utterly right.

"Oh, oh, oh...*now*." He released inside her with a long sigh of ecstasy and Holly experienced her *own* personal ecstasy to know she'd delivered him there. When his body finally stilled, she pulled his head to her chest and stroked his hair while he rested. And somehow, even on the kitchen floor, this felt...like it made all the sense in the world, like everything was right.

So it surprised her when, a moment later, he looked up and whispered, "Damn—I'm sorry."

She widened her eyes in surprise as she met his gaze. "Sorry? For what?"

"I..." he grinned sheepishly, "...usually have longer staying power."

She returned a half smile. Okay, maybe it *had* been a little quick. But the passion had made up for it enough that she hadn't even noticed. "What happened?" she asked sweetly.

"*You* happened," he replied.

"Oh." The heat of a blush rose to her cheeks. "Well, I forgive you."

"I'll make it up to you," he promised. "Soon. *Really* soon."

When he shifted his weight a little, Holly began to actually *feel* the kitchen floor beneath her—only now that she was coming back down to earth did she notice how incredibly hard the ceramic tile was and that her back ached from lying on it. And in spite of that, she grinned.

"What are you smiling about?" he asked.

"I just—" she shook her head, "—can't believe we did it on the kitchen floor." And in fact, for the first time in her life, Holly felt like she was truly *living*, doing the kinds of things she *heard* about people doing, acting *spontaneously*. And so far, she didn't regret it a bit.

"I can't believe we did it, period," he said, laughing.

And her eyes widened in teasing accusation. "Why not?"

"Because I thought you didn't know me well enough."

"I don't," she confirmed, "but I made an exception."

He tilted his head, eyes gleaming. "And what did I do to rate such an honor?"

"Well," she pointed out, "you *did* fix my shelf. It would have been rude of me not to thank you."

They both laughed, and then he playfully nibbled at her breast.

When she responded with a small moan, and he said, "I've got a suggestion."

"What's that?"

He flashed a matter-of-fact look. "The floor was fun, honey, but my knees are killing me. Let's go get in bed."

As she bit her lip and glanced around the room, reality still coming back to her piece by piece, she caught a glimpse of the clock on the microwave above them. "It's not even seven o'clock," she said, laughing.

"Um, I wasn't suggesting we go there to sleep," he explained in a low rasp.

And she considered the suggestion for only a second before saying, "Race you."

DEREK WATCHED HER sleep. Her red-blonde hair cascaded over the pillow like a fan and he wanted to touch it. But he didn't want to wake her, so he only looked.

He still couldn't believe it. Any of it. One innocent-seeming phone call and a few minutes later he'd been on the floor with her.

He couldn't believe the wild side of her he'd seen tonight. It had been the most exciting sex of his life. Because he knew that Holly wasn't usually like that. Because he knew she'd been like that only for him.

For him, this woman had concocted a plan to lure him to her house. For him, this woman had bared her soul, and her body, in the most candid, open, arousing way he'd ever experienced. For him, this woman had even sent her child away for the evening.

That last one almost affected him as deeply as the innocent frankness she'd displayed—the way she'd just laid it all out and gone after what she wanted. Because only yesterday morning she'd told him that Emily was her first priority and that each night of her life was set aside to be spent with her daughter.

It made him feel important.

And it made him feel like a rat.

On one hand, he knew the complete abandon they'd experienced could never have taken place if Emily had been here crying and eating and wetting her diaper.

On the other, though, he felt like he was stealing something from them both. Sure, from his perspective, it was easy to say it was just one night and not a big deal— but Holly had made it clear that every night with Emily was valuable to her. So in effect, he'd tampered with time that they cherished, with a mother-child bond he knew nothing about.

He was crazy about the woman and this night had been so right, so perfect, all that he'd dreamed. But he hadn't wanted her to feel like she had to send her baby away just to be with him.

Or did he? Hell, it was all so confusing.

Even just being so crazy about her was confusing. That wasn't his usual way. Usually, he was all about casual fun and casual sex. But something about this didn't feel casual—inside him. And how the hell had something like that happened so quickly? After all, he'd just met her.

He leaned over and placed a feathery kiss on her forehead.

"Hmm?"

He hadn't meant to wake her, but he'd liked the light, airy way her voice had sounded just then. "Go back to sleep," he whispered.

Instead, though, she opened her eyes and smiled at him. Even in the darkness, he saw the lovely twinkle of green in her gaze.

"What are you smiling about *this time*?" he asked.

"Just thinking about tonight," she admitted.

He nodded against his pillow, not bothering to hide how he felt. "Well worth smiling over."

"Derek," she said, "I want you to know that…well, I've never done anything like this before."

"Anything like what?"

"Sleep with someone I hardly know."

"That's okay," he said. "I feel like I know you." He meant it. It came with the being crazy about her part.

"Or seduce someone," she added.

He tried to hold his grin inside, but admitted, "That part I knew."

"How?" she asked. "Because I was so bad at it?"

He chuckled. "No—actually you were pretty damn effective at it."

Then she tilted her head against the pillow, smiling softly. "Then how'd you know it was my first time?"

"Your eyes," he told her. "They kind of gave you away."

"What do you mean?" she asked on a blink.

"They just had this…really pretty, innocent kind of look in them."

"Oh…" Her voice sounded feathery and romantic.

"You should go back to sleep," he told her. "You have to work tomorrow."

"So do you," she pointed out.

He flashed a grin. "Yeah, but I'm the boss. I can go in late if I feel like it."

"Mmm," she said, sounding jealous. "That's a luxury I certainly don't have." Then a sigh snuck out. "God, how nice it would be to make my own schedule, to find a way to spend some more time with Em…"

Derek could practically hear her thoughts. "You miss her right now, don't you?"

Her sheepish look only added to his lingering guilt. "Well…yes. I mean, I had an incredible time with you tonight, but I still…"

"It's okay," he told her. "You're allowed to miss her."

She smiled at him from beneath sleepy eyelids.

Inspiring him to playfully add, "But I'll see if I can take your mind off it for a few minutes." Then he rolled over on top of her and lowered a warm, passionate kiss to her lips.

HOLLY GLANCED AT the clock next to the bed. Darkness

still loomed, but daylight fast approached. It was nearly five a.m. And still they kept wanting each other.

She shifted her gaze to the man below her as she sat on top, straddling him. His hands slid slowly up and down her thighs, adding to her heat as she began to move on him.

"Unh…" he breathed below her.

She undulated in small circles, her body gyrating rhythmically above him, and a small moan escaped her as well. And soon she found herself moving harder, pressing her palms against his stomach for balance.

"Ohhh…" he groaned.

She leaned her head back as a tingling, excruciatingly sexy pressure built inside her. And she let the impulses in her body take over, drive her, command her, as the sensations grew more intense and the circles tighter and hotter.

"Aw baby…" he whispered up into the air.

And, mmm, his sexy voice was all she needed. The pleasure broke over her like crashing waves, pounding at her body, filling her with power yet taking all her control, then finally calming, quieting, delivering her to the smoothest, sweetest tranquility she had ever known.

She collapsed on Derek and breathed her satiated exhaustion into his chest.

After which he began to stroke her hair, whispering, "Was it nice?"

In reply, she bit her lip, then kissed his neck. "Mmm. Very."

"I'm glad."

Only a restful moment later, he started to thrust sweetly into her again. And she raised herself above him just slightly so that she could sprinkle his chest with light kisses. When the kisses turned to playful nips and bites, he moaned, his drives becoming deeper, harder. "Oh yeah," he rasped.

She raked her teeth across his chest once more, then lifted kisses to his neck, chin, mouth. And he murmured a heated "Mmm…" between more tiny kisses that grew warmer, stronger.

"I want you to do it," she whispered hotly in his ear.

"Oh God," he sighed, "I am."

And then she felt his release, heard him moaning his pleasure, and she let the sound saturate her soul.

She rested her head on his chest again, smiling devilishly inside to know that now *her* words, *her* voice, had pushed *him* over the edge. She'd never experienced this wholly bold, sexual side of herself before—and she was discovering that she enjoyed it.

She lifted her head to look into his eyes. "I kind of like surprising you that way," she admitted.

He flashed a sexy grin in the dark. "I kind of like it, too."

HOLLY MOVED AROUND the bedroom, getting dressed for work, watching Derek sleep. It was strange to be watching him instead of Emily. The sight warmed her heart with pleasant—not to mention hot—memories of the night they'd just shared. But something was missing, too. Her sweet little Em.

She tucked her blouse into her skirt, then reached for a dainty necklace. Facing the mirror, she flipped her hair over her shoulder and hooked the chain behind her neck.

That was when she heard the sheets rustle and glanced over to find Derek watching her with half-open eyes. One glimpse of him, rumpled and naked in bed, sent a fresh surge of desire rocketing through her already—wow, he looked good in the morning.

"Hi," he said with a sleepy-sexy smile.

"Hi," she returned, a warm blush rising to her cheeks, suddenly feeling timid. Without warning, she found herself biting her lip in embarrassment as she remembered some of the things she'd said and done last night. Looking back, she could scarcely believe her actions. But she'd been unable to help herself. He was a different kind of man than she'd ever known, and those differences had apparently brought out differences she'd never known about herself, too.

Derek's enticing morning smile and messy hair were nearly enough to send her diving back into bed with him. But she had to be sensible. The night was over and her real life and responsibilities called.

This must be how Cinderella felt at the ball. But it was way past midnight and Holly needed to do whatever she could to try and tie these two worlds—the world of last night, and the world of her real life—together.

"Can I make you some breakfast?" she asked.

He tilted his head to the side. "Sure you have time?"

She nodded. She'd only had to get one person ready today instead of two. "Bacon and eggs?"

"Mmm," he said. "That sounds like a better breakfast than I've had in ages."

"Well," she said, again feeling her own blush even as she spoke, "I want to replenish your strength."

Which brought a wicked grin to his face. "I lost count," he told her. "How many times?"

The heat in her cheeks increased, but she still met his warm gaze. "Four, I believe."

His eyes widened. "Damn, guess I *do* need my strength replenished then." He pushed back the covers and glanced over the side of the bed. "Uh, any idea where my underwear might be?"

"Probably in the kitchen," she said, still shocked by the truth, by the very words as they spilled from her lips. "Why don't you take a shower, and I'll make breakfast and, um…gather up your things."

He smiled. "Sounds like an offer too good to refuse."

She wasn't sure why she averted her eyes as he got out of bed and walked toward the bathroom. Old hints of her usual, more conservative self maybe. But when it hit her how silly that was now, she glanced around in time to catch a fabulous view of his butt, which looked, not surprisingly, as good as the rest of him. Her body tingled.

She felt as though she was floating on air as she padded to the kitchen, started the promised breakfast, then plucked Derek's clothing up from the floor, piece by piece. She put everything in a tidy pile just outside the bathroom door, still shocked by the entire event—and still pleasured by memories of it, as well.

A few minutes later, Derek appeared, dressed in the same clothes from last night. She looked up from the stove just in time to see him approach from behind, wrapping his arms warmly around her waist. "Thank you for last night," he breathed hot in her ear. "It was incredible."

And her stomach fluttered. "For me, too," she whispered above the crackling of bacon in the skillet.

"Can I help?" he asked about breakfast.

"No," she told him. "I've poured the juice and coffee—all I have to do is take up the bacon and eggs. Which, much as I regret it, will be easier without you wrapped around me."

He leaned in for a quick peck on the cheek, then retreated to the table in the dining room.

When they began to eat, he quickly complimented the food, which she appreciated. Bacon and eggs were simple, but a couple of meals with Derek were reminding her that it was nice cooking for someone besides herself. And it felt good to share a morning meal with someone who could answer her when she talked. She adored Emily's company, but adult conversation provided a different kind of satisfaction.

She watched him from across the table and wondered

how to bring up what she wanted to ask him. She had no idea what kind of response to expect. But the honest approach had certainly worked last night and she couldn't think of any other way.

"What are you doing tomorrow?" Which was Saturday.

He glanced up, a piece of bacon between his fingers. "Nothing special. Why?"

"Well, I was wondering if you'd like to go to the zoo with Emily and me."

Derek opened his mouth to answer—but then stopped, thinking it through.

He'd just spent an amazing night with this woman. And he'd also just about forgotten that Emily even existed. He hated the way it made him feel to suddenly remember her—but he couldn't help it. The image of himself pushing a stroller didn't hold much appeal. In fact, after the wild abandon he'd experienced with Holly last night, it seemed like an impossible picture—like two opposite ends of the spectrum.

"I…don't know," he finally told her, hesitating and feeling a little put on the spot.

"Oh," she said, suddenly sounding nervous and uncertain.

And—shit. Guilt gripped him by the throat. He didn't want to be a jerk here, didn't want to make her uncomfortable, so he should try to explain himself. But he didn't like admitting to her how he really felt about this. He'd look like just as big of a jerk *that* way, too.

And hell—quick as that, he found himself scrambling for an excuse. "I just remembered that I, um…have this thing I have to do tomorrow. In the afternoon. It slipped my mind."

He wished he could roll his eyes at his own lameness. He used to be a much smoother liar, but had gotten out of practice. And he was unable to read the change in Holly's expression.

"Oh, okay," she said. "No problem."

But as her eyes dropped to her plate, she sounded hurt, like a woman who knew when she was being lied to. And she also sounded tense, like a woman who didn't like it one bit.

His stomach sank. And for a second he considered backing things up and telling her he'd go to the zoo. But it just didn't feel right to him. He didn't want to play daddy to Emily and he didn't want to give Holly the impression that he did. He swallowed heavily, searching for some kind of an explanation, but his mind stayed blank—at least as far as coming up with anything convincing to say was concerned.

"It's…my friend," he finally managed. "I promised my friend that I would…do this thing. That's all." Still lame. Lame as hell.

And she didn't reply, but the look on her face told him that she either wanted to cry or to explode with anger.

"I'm sorry, Holly," he finally told her, his stomach churning with the weight of the moment.

Next to him, she took a deep breath. "No big deal," she said without meeting his eyes. Then she shoved a forkful of scrambled eggs into her mouth, her gaze planted squarely on the napkin holder that set between them on the table.

Shit. How had things turned so cold and awkward so quickly? He suddenly had a feeling that it would be better for both of them if he just left.

Quickly shoving the last bite of a strip of bacon into his mouth, he pushed back his chair and stood up. "I should go."

She didn't protest, but instead simply nodded and continued eating.

Derek walked to the door, and when he reached it, he stopped to look back at her with a sigh. He wanted to say something, do something—anything—to somehow try and fix what he'd just single-handedly destroyed. He couldn't believe he'd shared such an earth-shattering night of passion with her and had now managed to blow the whole thing already.

"I'm sorry about the zoo, Holly," he said again.

"I told you, it's no big deal," she replied, her tone suddenly almost snappish as she rose from the table herself. "Now I have to hurry, or I'll be late. Goodbye." And with that, she moved briskly toward the hallway, retreating to leave him standing in the living room alone.

He lingered there for a moment longer, hearing the silence of the house all around him. And he didn't like leaving things this way, but since she'd walked off, he didn't have much choice. He stepped out onto the porch feeling like an ass.

Thinking of their wild sex, of her sweet and sexy seduction, and then recalling her admission that she'd never done anything like that before, he let out another sigh. No wonder he felt like a jerk. She'd given him everything. All of herself.

And what had he given her in return? Not a damn thing.

Well, hot sex, yeah. *Really* hot sex—at times frantic and urgent, and at other times slow and sizzling. But for a guy like him...well, sex was easy. It was other things that came harder. And he had a feeling that for a woman like Holly, the sex was the part that took some...some changing, some opening up.

The worst part, though, was that he still thought he'd made the right call. Maybe a lady with a baby couldn't understand that not everybody wanted that in their life. Maybe she couldn't see how much having a baby involved would effect and define their relationship.

It didn't make him a bad guy—he just wasn't into playing daddy, and pretending he was, even for just one day, seemed like a bad idea. For all of them.

Chapter Eight

HOLLY STOMPED UP to the door of the daycare center. Then she stomped inside. She'd been stomping all day.

She couldn't believe she'd ditched Emily for a night with a man who, who…well, she guessed his only real crime was succumbing to her ridiculous forwardness. She'd just never thought about the morning after or what it would be like. She'd just never imagined that two people could be that excruciatingly intimate and into each other without there being something more to follow it.

How could a night be so perfect and then—poof—everything goes up in smoke. She'd let him see her at her most vulnerable, her most private, and…well, maybe the really terrible part, now that she thought through it, was that after her little scene this morning, they'd probably be something like enemies now. People who avoided each other. Because she'd probably seemed unreasonable. She wished she hadn't let her feelings show, but she'd been unable to hold them in.

She looked around impatiently. Where was Emily? She was dying to see her daughter after being away from her for so long. She scanned the area, filled with babies, toddlers, and preschoolers at play, but she didn't see Em anywhere.

That was when Miss Carol came from the back room, cradling a red-faced Emily in her arms.

"What's wrong?" Holly asked, rushing to take the baby.

"Nothing serious," Miss Carol assured her with a smile. "Emily's just been a little fussy today. Not her usual, pleasant self."

Holly's heart sank. Emily had been crying all day and Holly hadn't been here to comfort her. "Mommy's here, now, Em," she said, bending to kiss the baby's forehead and pull her close. "Mommy's here and everything's okay."

Taking in the look of contentment that grew on the baby's face, Holly raised her eyes to Emily's caretaker. "Thank you, Miss Carol. Have a good weekend." Then she located Emily's diaper bag and exited the building, ready to spend some quality time with her.

"Tonight it'll be just me and you, sweetheart," Holly said in her rearview mirror toward where Emily perched in her car seat. Emmy returned the gaze in the little pink mirror Holly had mounted in the backseat that enabled them to see each other while Holly drove. "We'll have a special night," Holly promised. "We'll have some applesauce and some strained peas—I know how you

love those. And then we'll sing some songs and play with
some toys and Mommy will read you a story from your
big Winnie-the-Pooh book. How's that sound?"

"Eh goo," Emily replied.

Holly smiled into the mirror. It felt good, safe, right,
to be back with her little girl again—and Holly regretted
having deserted her, even if it *had* been only for one
night.

HOLLY HAD JUST changed Emily into a pretty pink
summer sleeper, ordered a pizza for herself, and was
about to commence on the night of fun she'd put
together in her mind for her daughter. She'd also promised herself that she wasn't going to spoil the evening by
thinking about Derek.

Although she wondered just what his *thing* was tomorrow. And she figured that his *friend* was probably the
lingerie-wearing tramp she had envisioned last night
before she'd called to ask him over. The most horrible
part was that even if some other woman *was* in the
picture, Holly couldn't completely justify her own rage at
him. After all, she'd been the mad seductress—what had
she expected him to do?

Perhaps it was like this for most people. Perhaps the
whole world of single adults slept with one person one
night and someone else the next. She, for one, would
never be able to live that way. Still, she supposed it was
her own fault for getting in this deep—she'd given him

the perfect one-night stand, no questions asked.

Though Holly knew the more likely scenario was that his *friend* was a pure fabrication. Maybe he just didn't want to be with her. Maybe he didn't want to be with Emmy, either.

She hadn't exactly asked him to sign up for a lifetime commitment to either of them before sleeping with him, yet the idea still hurt. Enough that she instantly resolved not to think about it. And besides, she was breaking her own rule by letting him invade her mind.

She glanced down at Emily, who lay on a quilt on the living room floor peering up at her. "Come here, Em," she said, lifting the baby into her lap on the couch. She peered down into her eyes, still feeling guilty about finding her red-faced and teary-eyed earlier. "I apologize for taking you over to Aunt Michelle's last night, sweetie. Mommy didn't mean to abandon you. She just…needed some time."

Holly looked away for a moment, then turned her gaze back on her daughter. Part of her was caught up in remembering just what she'd done with that needed time, and just how wonderful it had been. But she still felt neglectful, considering how things had turned out in the end.

"Bubbubbubbub." Emily reached up to play with a button on Holly's blouse.

And despite herself, remembering that ending once more flooded Holly with depression. She knew a lot of it had been her own fault, but that didn't change how much Derek had hurt her this morning.

Bored with the button, Emily switched her glance to Ecyore, who sat nearby. Holly reached for the stuffed animal, handing him to Emmy with a deep sigh.

Last night had pushed her over a certain edge. No man had ever made her feel the things Derek Cassidy had when they'd made love. And while it had been stupendous sex—sex beyond anything she'd ever envisioned in her wildest dreams—it had also been something more. There had been emotion involved. At least on her part. She cared for him.

But no, care isn't the right word.

Irritation bit at her as she looked down at Emily and tried to sort her feelings out.

It wasn't the same as what she felt for Em, of course, but there were similarities. The same tender ache in her heart when she thought of something hurting him. The same brilliant energy when she thought of him smiling, laughing, being happy. She suffered the same need to hold onto him, to reach out to him, to cherish him.

Oh. I know what this is.

I love him.

But oh God! Wait! I love him? Is that even possible? Can it really happen that fast?

Then she took a long, deep breath, thought it through, and faced the facts.

It was true. She'd fallen in love with him.

She didn't like it. She didn't want it to be that way. She could scarcely think of any worse news at the moment.

"But I love him," she whispered.

She was rescued from her own thoughts when she heard a car pull in the driveway. Letting out a sigh, she lay the baby back on the quilt and rose to get her wallet.

She opened the front door a moment later, expecting to see the pizza guy, but instead she found Michelle approaching briskly up the walk, looking harried and upset. What could be wrong? Holly stepped out on the porch and rushed to close the distance between her sister and herself.

"What is it?" Holly asked.

"It's Mom," Michelle said, reaching out to squeeze Holly's hand. "She's had a heart attack."

Holly's *own* heart dropped to her stomach. This couldn't be!

But oh, damn it, of course it could. The chest pains she'd experienced—it all made sense. "How bad?" she asked Michelle.

"I don't know." She shook her head. "I just got a call from the hospital. We need to go."

Holly glanced forlornly back toward the door, thinking of Emily—and Michelle read her mind. "I left the kids with Rob," she said. "Is there a neighbor or someone who could watch Emmy?"

"I really hate to leave her," Holly responded quickly.

"We could be there all night," Michelle warned.

And Holly let out a heavy sigh, the whole situation weighing on her. Of course, she could only think of one person to call. But her stomach twisted at the very idea of asking him.

DEREK SAT DOWN in front of the TV with a can of beer and a bologna sandwich. There was a baseball game coming on. He didn't particularly feel like watching it, but he had to find some way to occupy himself. He had the whole night ahead of him and not a damn thing to do. "Pathetic," he mumbled.

"Meow," Claws echoed from somewhere in the room.

"Hey, you don't have to be so quick to agree," Derek chided him.

Claws revealed himself then, peeking up at Derek from beneath the end table next to the couch.

"Come on up here and keep your provider company," he told the cat. Then he reached down and grabbed the kitten, pulling him up onto the cushion next to him.

The fact that he was suddenly desperate enough for company to be talking to the cat again made him think of Holly. After all, since when did he mind time alone? Usually, he was fine with that and enjoyed quiet evenings unwinding from a day on the job. But now he suffered the odd, nagging feeling that there was someplace he should be, someone he should be spending his time with.

"Only it's not you," he told Claws, reaching to scratch the kitten behind the ears. "No offense."

And it surprised him to realize that the thought included more than just Holly. Despite his feelings this morning, and even despite the fabulous evening he'd spent alone with Holly last night, for some reason the picture in his head included Emily.

He didn't know why. It hardly made sense. Being alone with Holly, making mad passionate love to her all night long, had been a perfect dream come true. And still, when he imagined himself spending time at Holly's house, he saw Emily being there, too.

"I'm an ass," he said aloud, remembering the way things had ended this morning, the stupid lie he had told her. That was why he was alone right now when he'd rather be with her. That was why he was eating bologna.

"Meow."

"Again," he told the cat, "you didn't have to agree. I could use a little support right now."

Claws hopped silently onto Derek's leg and settled in his lap and—hell, one more surprise—he found himself taking a little comfort in the cat's presence. At least he *had* a cat.

"Wanna go for a walk?" he asked Claws, swallowing down the last of his sandwich.

"Meow."

Maybe he and Claws would…very casually stroll next door or something. See if anybody was home and if he could do something to make up with the lady next door.

The fact was, from the beginning, he'd had it bad for her. This hadn't been normal from the word go. So maybe his confusion—not to mention his complete flip-flopping on the issue—only made sense in a way. He kept trying to back away, for good reasons. At least they seemed like good ones to him. But he couldn't deny that he was having a hard time with that, and at the moment he was going to follow the path of least resistance and see where it led.

He nudged Claws until he pounced to the carpet below. Then he went to the door and held it open, a late summer breeze wafting inside.

The cat trotted merrily out the door and Derek followed. The scent of fresh-mown grass from someone's lawn made him feel refreshed and energized. And ready to maybe undo what he'd so impulsively done this morning.

Now, we have to be subtle. Casual. Nonchalant.

But where was Claws? Derek darted his head around in time to see a streak of white go dashing across the yard toward Holly's house to where she stood outside with another lady. He sighed. So much for subtlety.

"Meow."

He watched as Holly glanced down at the miniature white cat who rubbed up against her ankle.

"Come here, Claws," he said, approaching. He felt a little embarrassed, as if he'd sent the cat over to mediate. "Sorry," he said, hurrying to scoop up the kitten, then taking a step back. "I guess I need to get him a leash if I'm gonna take him on walks."

Only when Holly didn't respond did he realize that her face was fraught with despair. And it was more than a being-mad-at-him despair like this morning. It was more of a frantic despair. The woman standing beside her wore the same expression. "Holly, what's wrong?" he asked.

"My mother," she said. "She just had a heart attack."

His chest tightened at the news. "Oh God—I'm sorry." The words, her expression—it instantly took him back to when he'd gotten the call about Aunt Marie and he wished for some way to comfort her.

"I have to go to the hospital," she told him, sounding dazed.

"Do you want me to stay with Emily?" he asked automatically.

Holly took a deep breath upon hearing the unexpected offer. *Did she want him to stay with Emily?* This time her doubts had nothing to do with fearing for Emily's safety—Derek had proven himself a trustworthy babysitter the other night. No, this time she feared for herself.

His dark eyes were so warm on her, so filled with concern—and this morning's rift seemed to have faded. But did she want to be indebted to this man? Did she want to risk growing more attached? Could she bear to come home and find him sitting in her living room looking so gorgeous and sexy when she knew there was no future between them?

Still—Michelle was right. It wasn't practical for Emily to spend the entire night at the hospital with them, and Holly barely felt capable of taking care of her child at the moment, anyway. Her mother had just had a heart attack, after all—she felt as if she could barely take care of herself.

"Are you…sure?" she asked him.

He nodded, and their eyes met and held.

But you can't think about him right now, or anything that's happened between you. This was no time to be analyzing her love life. "Follow me," she said.

She headed in the house with Derek on her heels to where Emmy still lay on the quilt. "She hasn't eaten," she told him. "There are strained peas and applesauce sitting out on the kitchen counter. And I just made up a bottle."

"Okay," he said, nodding.

"I changed her diaper a little while ago, but she'll probably need it again after she eats."

"Got it."

"If she cries and you can't figure out why," she went on, shoving a pacifier into his hand, "try this."

"Everything will be fine," he assured her.

Holly moved back toward the door, but before stepping outside, she stopped and turned back to Derek. She hated herself for the warmth she felt for him in that moment, but it was something she couldn't push down. She leaned toward him and placed her hands on his shoulders, then gave him a quick kiss. "Thank you," she whispered.

Derek watched her run from the house, still feeling the sensation of her velvet-soft lips on his. When she reached the car, she stopped and looked back at him, standing at the door. "I forgot—I've a got a pizza on the way." A troubled expression clouded her already distressed face as she started to dig in her purse.

"No worries—I'll pay for it," he told her. "Go."

He watched her drive away with the woman he guessed to be her sister, then he looked down at Claws, who he still held in one hand. "Okay, I admit it," he said to the cat. "This isn't exactly what I was hoping for." Then he glanced over to the pink-clad baby on the quilt. "But this won't be so bad. I did it before, I can do it again. Unfortunately for you, though, I'm not sure I can babysit and catsit at the same time, so I think I'm gonna have to send you home for the evening."

DEREK TOOK A bite of pepperoni pizza. Then he spooned some green goo—supposedly strained peas—into Emily's mouth.

She smiled at him just before half the spoonful of green stuff came oozing back out through her tiny lips. He used the spoon to catch the overflow and pushed it gently back inside. After that, he took another bite of pizza.

"How are those peas, Emily?" he asked.

"Gaaaa," she replied.

He nodded. Then suggested, "How about some applesauce, now. Your mom said you should have both."

Dipping the tiny baby spoon into the small jar of applesauce, he slid it between her lips. And she accepted it—but also twisted her expression into a slight grimace.

"I never liked applesauce much, either," he confided in her. "But we have to do what your mom said." He followed that by shoveling another small spoonful of it into her mouth and watching her swallow it.

"Good girl," he told her, offering a slight grin. He supposed she was a pretty cute baby.

He continued to feed Emily while he ate pizza. And he interspersed the baby food with drinks of formula from the bottle Holly had left. He didn't know if that was the right way to do it, but he figured Emily might need some help washing down that applesauce. She liked the green stuff much better.

He fed her until she seemed disinterested—she'd downed about half a jar of each of her courses. Then he reinserted the bottle into her mouth and watched her drink the rest of her dinner. So far so good.

"Well, Emily," he said when she'd finished her bottle, "looks like it's you and me for a while."

"Ah gooo."

And he realized that *a while* could even be all night. He hoped he could do a satisfactory job of taking care of her if it turned into an overnight thing.

Again, he sort of wished there was someone he could call for help if he needed it. Maybe Holly would check in by phone at some point, and if he had any questions, he could ask her then. But at the same time, he wanted to seem capable here. He didn't want her to have to worry about anything besides her mother.

An hour later, he'd successfully changed Emily's diaper, cleaned up the dinner mess, and put the remainder of the pizza in the fridge. He felt like he was doing a good job. So it figured that, just when he was starting to feel comfortable, Emily would break into tears.

He sat on the couch, cradling her in his arms and peering helplessly down into her scrunched up eyes as tears streamed down her little face. "Waaaaaa! Waaaaa! Waaaaaa!"

What the hell could be wrong? He'd changed her diaper just a little while ago. And he'd fed her just before that. He wasn't sure what else to check.

Then he remembered the pacifier Holly had given him on the way out the door. Leaning over, he plucked it up from where he'd set it on the coffee table and gently nudged it into her open, crying mouth.

Silence filled the room as Emily grabbed onto the pacifier with her lips and sucked wildly.

Whoa. Amazing!

Emily closed her eyes and enjoyed whatever comfort the pacifier provided as Derek watched the rapid sucking motions of her mouth, noting how pleased she looked, how suddenly peaceful. He couldn't help smiling.

"Is that what you wanted?" he asked her.

She opened her eyes and looked up at him, continuing to pull at the pacifier.

"I guess it was."

It occurred to him then that night had fallen—it was dark outside, and he and Emily were all alone. And all in all, everything was fine. "We do all right, you and me, don't we?" he asked the baby.

She didn't answer, of course.

But he thought that if she could, she'd agree.

Chapter Nine

HOLLY SQUEEZED HER mother's hand, then turned to leave the room. Visitors were being admitted one at a time and it was Michelle's turn.

"How is she?" her sister asked when Holly came out into the hall in the intensive care unit.

"Weak," Holly replied. "But she spoke to me, asked me where Emily was." Holly smiled tiredly about her mother's concern for the baby even in her own critical condition and Michelle did, as well.

"By the way," Michelle said, "I was too upset to ask you before, but was that the hunk?"

Holly nodded.

Her sister leaned forward just slightly. "And last night, did you?"

Holly nodded again.

Michelle's eyes brightened amid her worry. "And was it great?"

Holly nodded a third time, but she knew her disheartened expression required an explanation. Only she couldn't give one now. "It was…beyond amazing—but it didn't end well. Long story. For another time."

Michelle nodded and patted her shoulder. "I'm gonna go in now."

Holly stood outside and waited for her sister, trying to remember everything the doctor had told them. Her mother was in critical but stable condition. Chances for recovery were good, but she wasn't completely out of the woods yet.

The doctor had suggested that she and Michelle go home after they each visited with their mother for a few minutes, but they planned to stay. Critical but stable didn't sound totally reassuring and they both wanted to be there if their mother needed them.

Then Holly thought of Emily and Derek. Even after he'd offered, she'd still felt bad accepting his help. Because the more she played his feeble excuse about tomorrow over in her head, the more certain she became that he just hadn't wanted to spend time with her and Emmy.

Maybe she was just mad at herself. For what she'd wanted. Because wasn't that *exactly* what she'd been hoping for—that Derek would want her and Emily *both* in his life?

But it was a lot to ask of a single man, perhaps more than was reasonable, especially this soon after meeting him. After all, having a baby certainly hadn't been *his* decision.

And yet she knew she couldn't be with a man who couldn't embrace Emily as part of the deal.

Why did it all have to be so complicated? Why couldn't she find some happy medium?

Because there isn't one.

After walking down the hall, Holly took a deep breath and dialed her own number.

"Hello?"

"Hi Derek—it's Holly."

"How's your mom?"

Another deep breath. "Stable."

"That's good news," he said.

"Yes," she replied. "How's Em doing?"

"We're fine," he told her. "We ate, we diapered, and now we're enjoying our pacifier."

And Holly couldn't help smiling. This didn't sound quite like a man who minded spending time with her daughter. "So things are going well?"

"Things are going great." She thought she even heard a hint of pride in his voice, which softened her heart toward him still more.

And she couldn't help it—the fact that he was making this so easy on her filled her with affection. It was a difficult night for her, and he *could* be making it worse— but instead he was making it better. "Derek, I don't know how to thank you for taking care of Emmy for me tonight."

"You don't have to," he said. "Really."

She bit her lip thoughtfully, glad he couldn't see the measure of appreciation on her face. Because, of course, it was more than just appreciation. It was love.

"So…" she began then, "would it trouble you too much…if I didn't come home quite yet?"

"No, not at all," he said. "Take as much time as you need."

"Are you sure? Because I *could* come home. But I just kind of want to be here, you know, just in case…"

"Holly," he said, his deep voice enough to weaken her knees even over the phone, "I don't mind. Honest. I can stay as long as you need me to."

She sighed, then spoke very softly. "Thank you. Thank you for being so sweet."

"I can't help myself," he said playfully. "It's just the kind of guy I am."

And she found herself wishing the distance that lay between them would somehow just magically disappear, the distance between here and home—and other kinds of distance, too.

DEREK KNEELED BEFORE Emily on the quilt on the living room floor and watched her still working away on her beloved pacifier. "Ahgooooo," she cooed, flipping the pacifier out of her mouth.

It made him laugh, and he reached out to tickle her stomach. And when she offered a soft giggle in return, their eyes met. *Such little eyes. But still so expressive.* He had a strange impulse to pick her up—but he ignored it. She was doing fine where she was.

"You want this back?" he asked, offering the pacifier

again.

She accepted it into her mouth and returned to her sucking motions.

In search of some additional way to entertain her, he reached around behind him and found Eeyore. "Here's Eeyore," he said, holding the purple donkey up where Emily could see. Maybe he imagined it, but he could have sworn her eyes brightened. "Eeyore loves you," he said—and then he touched the stuffed animal's mouth to Emily's nose while he made a kissing sound.

Wait. Eeyore loves you? Where was he getting this stuff? And he'd be pretty damn embarrassed if anyone else was around. But they weren't, thank goodness.

Emily sneezed then and the pacifier shot from her mouth like a bullet and whacked Derek in the forehead.

"Hey!" he said.

But Emily just lay below him laughing.

"Oh, that's funny, huh?" he asked, smiling down at her. Then he tried to picture it in his mind—him getting hit with a flying pacifier. "Yeah," he agreed, "I guess it *was* pretty funny."

The two of them played with Eeyore for a little while, then switched off to a white stuffed rabbit he found sitting in her swing. He made the rabbit hop up Emily's leg and across her stomach before letting it kiss her. She smiled each time. And soon he found himself making funny faces at her—widening his eyes and opening his mouth as if in great surprise. Every once in awhile he stopped and shook his head, though, growing even more thankful Emily was the only person here to witness his behavior.

A little after ten o'clock, she began to cry. He checked her diaper, but it was dry. And then he tried the pacifier—to no avail. Even Eeyore and the bunny had lost their magic. "Maybe you just miss your mommy," he said, carefully lifting her off the quilt and into his arms. He walked around the room, rocking her back and forth as he'd seen Holly do—and the tears slowed, but they didn't stop. "I do, too," he confessed.

It had been nice to hear Holly's voice on the phone. When she'd reported that her mother was in stable condition, he'd felt almost as relieved—for her sake—as if it had been Aunt Marie. He knew it was still very serious, but it sounded like the worst scare was over.

He sat down on the couch, Emily cradled in his arms. He wished she seemed more comforted by his holding her—somehow it comforted *him*—but her gentle cries continued. "Shhh, Em," he whispered.

"Waaaaaaa," she cried softly.

Derek remembered the time he'd heard Holly singing to Emily and how it had quieted her. But he didn't know the words to that mockingbird song people always sang to babies. In fact, he couldn't think of many baby songs at all—he wasn't sure any had ever been sung to *him*.

"Rock-a-Bye Baby," he said then, lifting a triumphant finger in the air as he remembered the lullaby.

Then he began. "Rock-a-bye baby, in the tree top.

When the wind blows, the cradle will rock. When the bow breaks, the cradle will fall..." He let his voice trail off then, though. *The cradle will fall?* That didn't exactly sound soothing. In fact, wasn't it kind of scary? Who made up these things? He wasn't going to sing the rest of it.

But Emily continued to cry softly, and as he reached a cloth up to dry some of her tears, he knew he needed to try something else. Only he didn't know any more lullabies. So...maybe he'd just sing her a song he knew. Which meant he had to *think* of a song he knew.

He knew lots of songs by the Rolling Stones. Aunt Marie had been a fan and it had sort of carried over. So after another moment's pondering, he began to sing to Emily again, rocking her in his arms. "I can't get no...sa-tis-fac-tion. I can't get no...strained pea action. Well, I cry, and I cry..." Thinking that part particularly suitable, he finished the chorus, then moved on the faster verse. "Well, I'm drinking from my bottle, and I think it might be empty, and I'm trying to get some milk. I can't get no...no, no, no. No strained pea action...no strained pea action..."

HOLLY ENTERED THE house quietly. Like the other night when she'd come home to Derek and Emily, the lights were low and all was quiet. A smile found her face when she spotted them—they both lay on the quilt, Emily asleep in the crook of Derek's shoulder. One of his arms wrapped protectively around the baby and in the other hand he held Eeyore. His eyes were closed, but he was tapping his bare toes on the carpet, so she knew he was awake. Despite what had happened between them that morning, Holly couldn't help feeling that she couldn't have left her daughter in better hands.

They looked so adorable that she almost didn't want to let Derek know she'd come home. But it was past midnight and she supposed she should end his shift.

"Hey," she said softly.

He slowly opened his eyes, and then gave her a soft smile. "Hey," he returned sleepily. "Didn't hear you come in."

"Sorry I'm so late," she apologized.

But he shook his head. "I told you, we're fine. Don't we look fine?" He turned to steal a glance at Emily.

And Holly grinned. "Yes, you look fine."

"Your mom's condition improving?" he asked, carefully sliding out from beneath the baby, gently lowering her head to the quilt.

Holly sat down on the couch, nodding. "She's much better. She'll be in the hospital for a few days, but they're expecting her to be okay."

"That's great," Derek said. "I was worried. For you."

Holly sighed as the strange, new, helpless love she felt for him coursed through her veins and his sweet concern fell over her like a warm blanket. "Thank you," she whispered.

"Well," he admitted softly, "I know what it's like to

lose someone you love."

Holly bit her lip. "Have you…lost someone recently?"

He rose from the quilt and joined her on the couch, and she was glad to be closer to him. "Yeah," he said. "My Aunt Marie. She passed away pretty suddenly—kidney failure."

"I'm sorry," Holly said.

"She was kind of like…a mother to me," he went on. "It happened just a couple months ago." Then he offhandedly pointed in the direction of his house. "That's how I ended up next door to you."

And then Holly suddenly remembered the nice, older lady who had lived in the house before Derek. "Marie next door was your aunt?"

"Yeah. You knew her?" His eyes lit up when he asked.

"Just a little. We'd say hello in passing," she added, smiling. "And she brought over a casserole when Bill died. I didn't know what happened to her—I don't really know any of the neighbors well enough to ask." Then she shook her head. "I'm really sorry to hear that she's gone."

Derek shrugged as Holly knew men were sometimes wont to do in times of sorrow, trying to play it off as no big deal. But then his eyes grew distant, as if he was seeing something she couldn't, and she sensed a heavy weight about him that she hadn't just a moment before. She had the urge to reach out, touch him, but she didn't want to embarrass him. So instead she just whispered, "Are you all right?"

"I'm sorry," he said, visibly trying to shake off his sorrow. "I guess I just…miss her. I try not to think about it. But I pretty much owe her my life."

His words caught her wholly off guard. And she didn't want to pry, but she had to ask. "You owe her your life?"

He simply met her gaze, his eyes filled with emotion she couldn't read. And she wanted, more than anything in that moment, to know his secrets.

"Holly," he began then on a deep sigh, "there's so much you don't know about me."

"Well, of course. We just met," she reminded him.

"But it doesn't quite feel that way, does it?" he asked with a frank tilt of his head.

"No," she replied. And finding out he felt that way, too, somehow made *all* her feelings for him somehow seem a little safer. Like the connection she felt to him was more than one-sided—like it was something real, and important.

"Still," he went on, "there's so much you'd be…surprised to know. Things you might not *want* to know."

The words made her heart pump faster—with curiosity, and maybe even a little fear. He *did* have secrets. What were they? On impulse, she reached for his hand. "You can tell me."

He looked away—toward the window, as if maybe he

was considering a means of escape—but then his eyes dropped briefly to Emily, his expression softening just slightly, before he raised them back to her. "I never knew my mother," he told her.

"Oh Derek," she breathed. "Why not?"

"She ran off when I was a baby."

Holly stayed silent, something inside her shriveling as his words sunk in. How could any mother do that to her child? It was beyond her ability to grasp.

"My dad was a drunk," he added simply then.

And she squeezed his hand, wishing for some better way to comfort him. Seeing glimpses in his eyes of the little boy he'd once been broke her heart all the more.

"And he was the kind of drunk who…well, let's just say he sort of took out his frustrations on me, used me as a punching bag."

At this, she lifted her free hand to cover her mouth, trying to hold in her gasp. And she blinked, trying to will away a deeper reaction, but a tear rolled down her cheek anyway. She wiped it away, wanting desperately to hug him, but somehow she knew he wouldn't want that kind of hug, wouldn't *want* her to see him as a little boy who needed that.

"Aunt Marie was my mother's sister," he explained. "We weren't in contact while I was a kid, but then one day she saw my dad somewhere and asked about me. She came over to our house and saw how we lived, which was, basically, in squalor. And she decided to get me out of there."

"I'm so glad," Holly breathed.

He met her gaze. "Me, too," he whispered. Then his voice came back to normal. "Dad didn't put up much of a fuss—the only reason he regretted seeing me go was not having anybody to boss around anymore. Aunt Marie brought me here to live—" he pointed again, "—to her house. I was twelve and, by that time, a pretty rotten kid. I put that woman through hell when I was a teenager."

Holly tilted her head. "What did you do?"

He glanced down, seeming unable to meet her eyes.

And she again said, "You can tell me. I'll understand."

But this time he shook his head. "Don't take this the wrong way, but honey, you don't seem like the kind of girl who...*could* understand the kind of life I've led. That's not your fault—I just doubt you were exposed to the kinds of shit I was. And no kid should go through the things I did. But...I wasn't the same guy I am now. I barely know you and I'm still pretty sure our lives were pretty damn different. So I'm...not sure you *will* understand."

"Listen," she told him, "my mom and dad divorced when I was ten years old, and that's rough on any kid. By the time I was fifteen, we never even saw him. So it wasn't all wine and roses for me, either. And I'm sure it wasn't nearly as bad as what you went through, but...just try me. I might understand more than you think."

Derek took a deep breath. He couldn't believe he was

telling her *any* of this. He hadn't really talked to anyone in his life about it, ever—not his friends, not guys he worked with, not women he dated. And he meant what he'd said—he wasn't sure she'd get it and it might change the way she saw him.

And yet, it was pouring out of him easier than he could have imagined. And despite himself, he almost *wanted* to tell her, wanted her to know. Because if he was gonna care about this woman…well, maybe it was a matter of seeing if she could care about him back. All of him. Scars and all.

"I got into drugs in high school," he said. Then he stopped, waiting for her reaction—but when he got none, he went on.

"I hung with a rough crowd—I didn't really know any way to be but bad. Guess all I knew was that I didn't want to spend the rest of my life getting beat up like I had as a kid, so I wanted to seem like the kind of guy who'd *do* the beating up." He paused, again anticipating some kind of response, but it still didn't come.

But he still had worse stuff to throw at her. "I started shoplifting then. It was a game with my friends and me—we dared each other to steal things. And then we even started breaking in places at night—businesses where they didn't have security cameras or anything to stop us besides maybe a lock or two. I got caught and ended up in juvenile detention for six months when I was sixteen."

At some point, his gaze had shifted back to the window as he'd spoken—from shame maybe, because the man he'd become sure as hell didn't like remembering the troubled boy he'd been—but when he finished, he took a deep breath and made himself look at her again. She still said nothing, but...well, she didn't appear *completely* horrified. Though he hoped he was reading her right.

"When I came home," he went on, "Aunt Marie set me straight. She told me if I didn't clean up my act, lose my punk friends, and 'fly right'—as she put it, that she'd make sure I went back to juvy and stayed there until I was eighteen. She said I wouldn't amount to anything unless I saw the good in myself and changed right then. That moment, she said, was the most important one I'd ever had. She said it would make or break the rest of my life, and that I had a big decision to make—that I could take a shot at a decent life or I could ruin it for good."

"And?" Holly prodded.

He let his expression soften. "I took a shot at a decent life."

Holly smiled at him. "I kind of thought so."

"You did?"

"Well, yeah," she said. "Because look at you now."

Though he tilted his head, truly curious. "What do you see?"

"An intelligent, ambitious, responsible, and reliable man," she told him.

And he raised his eyebrows, sincerely surprised. "You see all that?"

"Not the first moment we met, no," she said. "But a few days in, I think I'm able to read between the lines."

And with that, Holly reached up and cupped his cheek in her hand, appreciating the late day stubble there, then she leaned over and kissed him. His mouth opened gently against hers and she let his tongue slide inside and turn in warm, soft circles around her own. Everything else—what had already happened between them, whatever might or might not happen now—mattered nothing to her in that moment. She'd been drawn to him in an inescapable way and kissing him had felt like the most natural, right, honest thing to do in the world, so she'd simply done it.

"Mmmmm," he breathed when the kiss ended. "I wasn't sure I'd ever get to do that again."

"Why not?" she asked.

"Well," he said, "for one thing, you don't seem like the type of woman who goes around kissing criminals. Or letting them take care of your baby."

"You're not a criminal," she said. "You're not the boy you used to be."

"I'm glad you know that," he told her. "But for another thing, after this morning I didn't think you'd ever want to see me again. I owe you an apology, honey. I acted like a jerk."

"I thought *I* owed *you* an apology," she admitted. "For getting mad so easily. Even if I'm pretty sure you don't really have anything to do with a friend tomorrow."

He released a heavy breath, a look of shame reshaping his eyes. "Guilty as charged," he said, voice low.

But she didn't want him to feel ashamed. Given the things he'd just told her, she suspected he'd already done his time in the shame department. And she wished he hadn't lied, but looking back, she supposed she'd put him on the spot a little.

So she decided to say the thing she really feared, because she wanted to clear the air and get to the heart of the matter. And whatever the answer, she'd act mature about it and not go running off into the other room. "Derek, is the reason you lied to me because you don't want to be saddled with a baby?"

"Holly," he said, his strong jaw clenching a little, "it's not about being saddled. It's about…"

"What?"

He stared off into the distance once more, for only a few seconds this time, and then he turned to peer into her eyes. "It's about me," he told her. "It's about what I envisioned for my life. When I finally grew up and started taking some responsibility for myself, I got a picture in my head of what I hoped my life would be. I knew I wanted to start my own business. And I hoped that somewhere down the road I'd make enough money to buy nice things and eventually have somebody to share them with."

"Oh," she said, thinking she got the picture now. After all, he had started the story nicely enough, but he hadn't finished the equation the same way she would have. "No children," she said.

He lowered his chin in a quick nod. "That's...how I always pictured my life."

Her stomach dropped at the news. Because this meant her fears were founded. And that it wasn't just about right now—it was about...forever. Her lips began to tremble, but she forced another question out anyway. "Is there...a reason why?"

He sighed and told her, "There are a *hundred* reasons why. Starting with my own parents. I never had a mother, and for all practical purposes, I never had a dad, either."

"But that doesn't mean—"

He held up a hand to stop her. "Please," he said. "Let me finish. Holly, I can't be a parent to a child. I can barely take care of myself. I never had role models—I don't even know what a good parent is supposed to be, or do."

"You could learn," she protested.

"That's not it," he argued. "Or...maybe that's *exactly* it."

"Huh?"

"It shouldn't be something that you have to talk yourself into—it should come naturally. Like with you and Emily." He ran his hands back through his hair. "Honey, I'm just not cut out to have kids. I can't be responsible for shaping a child's view of the world. I'm not prepared. I don't have the answers and I never will. I'm just not...parent material."

"But Derek—"

"Wait," he told her. "But Derek nothing. It's just how things are. I mean, it's the way I feel. I can't help it—that's me, who I am." He looked deeply into her eyes, as green and crystalline as ever. As he spoke, he felt purged somehow of sins he didn't even fully grasp. And yet he wished he could be a different kind of man, the kind of man who could make her happy, who could want to be a father to her child. "I understand," he concluded, "why you got upset this morning. And I understand if you're upset with me right now. I'll also understand if…you don't want to see me anymore."

"I *do* want to see you, Derek," she told him. "But I'm also not sure…how I can do that, considering Emily."

He nodded. Obviously, he knew as well as she did that Emily had to be her first priority.

"You see, when I got pregnant with Emmy, the plan was for me to stay home to raise her. Then, when Bill died, all that changed."

"How *did* Bill die?" he asked gently.

"A car accident," she replied.

"I'm really sorry," he told her then, his voice softening. And a heavy moment of silence hung between them until he quietly added, "Holly, can I ask you a really personal question?"

She nodded. No matter how this conversation ended, and even though the outlook for it seemed grim, she still felt so close to him right now that she thought she'd tell him anything.

"Do you still love him?" Derek asked. "I mean, I'm sure you still love him, but are you still...*in love* with him?"

Holly considered the question. There was a right answer, a *proper* answer. And then there was...honesty. "I don't think so," she confessed in a whisper. "And maybe...maybe I never really was."

She watched the dark color of his eyes somehow deepen. "What do you mean?"

"Bill was...convenient for me," she explained. "And I was that way for him, too. Everyone we knew seemed to think we were the perfect couple and should get married. So we did. But there was...well, no great, enduring passion there."

And that was when something lit in Derek's eyes, something heated and intense, something so powerful that it forced her to look away.

Refocus. Keep being honest.

"I've never told anyone that before," she admitted. She stared down at her hands as she spoke—and then saw his larger hands come into view, capturing hers.

"Thank you for telling me," he whispered. "And...please don't feel bad about it. It's how you feel, Holly. You can't help that." The words reminded her of the same he'd spoken moments before, about himself, about his not wanting to have kids. And just for a moment, she understood. Because he was right—you truly *couldn't* help how you felt about the big things in life.

"Anyway," she said with a sigh, coming back to the huge dilemma before them, "not being able to stay home with Emmy has restructured my life, changed it from what I thought it would be. I spend all day missing her, Derek. And when I come home at night, I want to be with her. I want to watch everything she does, see every new expression on her face, see her smile and frown, listen to her make sounds and try to make words."

She paused, gathering the courage to return her gaze to his. "I...don't know how to have a relationship with a man right now," she told him. She felt stupid, but she didn't know how else to explain it.

"I understand," he told her, lifting a hand to her cheek.

"You do?"

He nodded. "But I don't know the answer. For you and me. We have...different things going on in our lives. We're in different places. I'm not sure..." He trailed off on a sigh.

"I know," she said softly. She didn't like acknowledging it, but she couldn't see any way around it, either.

Another silence grew between them, this one a little uncomfortable, and Holly realized they were both exhausted. It was the middle of the night. "Well, it's late," she said.

He nodded and they both stood up. He offered her a wistful smile through sleepy eyes. "Should I kiss you goodnight?"

"Would you like to?"

"Very much."

"Then I'd…like that, too."

She wrapped her arms around his neck and leaned into his masculine warmth. She wished she could stay there forever. Their lips met in a series of soft, sweet kisses that made her long to sleep in his arms.

But that just didn't seem possible. Because she was a package deal.

"Goodnight," she finally said.

"Goodnight," he told her. "And, um, call me if you need anything else. I mean that."

Nodding, she watched him leave, walking across the lawn and entering the house next door. And even when he'd shut out the night and lights began to go off, darkening his windows, she stood there watching, envisioning him inside, thinking of how they should be there, or here, together…*together*—but as they'd both agreed, it simply couldn't be.

He was so near, but so horribly far away.

Chapter Ten

EMOTIONAL EXHAUSTION HELPED Holly sleep well. In the morning, she awoke refreshed and ready to face the day.

Pushing back the covers, she got out of bed and went straight to Emily's room. It was Saturday and, while she knew she would spend some time at the hospital, she also planned to devote some quality time to Emmy today, too. To make up for the last couple of nights. And because seeing her daughter all weekend had become her primary motivation for making it though the work week.

"Morning, Em," Holly said, lifting the baby into her arms. Emily's eyes fluttered open and Holly smiled at her. "Time for breakfast, sweetie." After that, she planned on a bath in the kitchen sink and then dressing her in something pretty.

Carrying the baby to the kitchen, Holly lowered her to her bouncer seat on the floor. "Sorry our plans got cancelled last night," she said to Emmy as she went about preparing a bottle and pouring herself some cereal. "But it was an emergency."

"Ah goooo."

Thinking of last night created other memories for Holly, too. Derek's goodnight kisses still seemed fresh on her lips. And the things he'd told her about his past loomed fresh in her mind, as well.

She'd never felt so strung out or confused over a man in her life. He said he didn't want kids, but when she saw him with Emmy, well...her heart simply did a little flip flop. It was like her two favorite people were right in one place, snuggled up together, and it seemed perfect.

"Goooooo."

Emmy's cooing reminded her that yes, she'd only seen them together sleeping—so who knew what kind of chaos had taken place before they'd reached that point. But Holly didn't really think there *had been* any chaos. Derek had just looked so content with Emmy...

She let her thought trail off, wondering if she had any right to try to make him be a father when he'd blatantly told her he just didn't want to. After all, who was she to try to twist his life like that? Shouldn't it be *his* decision? Yet still, she knew if something didn't change on that front, their relationship was doomed.

DEREK ROLLED OVER in bed and faced the sunshine. What day was it? Saturday? He glanced at the clock on the nightstand. The glowing numbers read 9:30. Why on earth was he so tired this late in the morning?

Then he shot to a sitting position in the bed, the

memory hitting him hard.

He'd been up half the night with Holly. And he'd told her *everything*.

What could he have been thinking?

But as their late night talk started coming back to him more clearly, he remembered—he hadn't really *been* thinking. And the words had poured out of him so easily that he just hadn't bothered to stop them. He'd been so sleepy and it had been so simple to tell her.

Still, thinking about it made him feel a little sick. He'd managed to keep his past to himself his entire adult life—so why did he have to start talking about it now? What must she think of him? Drugs? Jail?

Of course, that was a long time ago and he was no longer the boy who'd done all those stupid things. But how could he expect her to understand that?

And yet, she *had* understood. She had held his hand; she had kissed away his painful memories.

It was beyond him to understand how a sweet woman like Holly could accept his past so easily, but she'd done it, no questions asked.

Just then Claws leaped up onto the bed and walked across Derek's stomach.

"Hey buddy," he said, petting the cat. "How was your night without me?"

"Meow."

"Sorry I had to ditch you, but it was an emergency."

Then he shook his head. The more he talked to Emily and Claws, the easier and more normal it started to seem. It struck him as ridiculous, and yet the conversation made him feel a sort of companionship, even if the conversation was only one-way. "Claws," he said, "thanks to you, *and* Holly, *and* Emily, I have definitely lost my edge."

After dragging himself out of bed, he freshened Claws' water dish and dumped some food into the bowl on the floor next to the refrigerator. Feeling generous, he even poured a little milk over the dry kitten food.

Well, at least the truth is out now. Although he'd never thought about it much, he supposed he'd always worried about the day when he'd meet a woman he really cared for—worried about telling her the truth about him. He still couldn't get over how easy it had been to tell Holly that truth. And her acceptance had followed just as effortlessly.

"I always thought saying it out loud would be the hard part," he mused as he watched Claws enjoy his milk-soaked food.

But despite telling her the truth, a much larger problem still loomed between them and he didn't know what to do about it.

The smart thing would be to forget it. To decide to be friends, neighbors. No kissing. No touching.

But he'd already tried that and it hadn't lasted long. Even now he knew it would be impossible—every time he saw her he wanted to touch her. And since going to bed with her, that feeling had only grown. He wished he could take her to bed right now.

He thought back on the way she had moved above him, her red-blonde hair falling down over her breasts, her breath coming so soft and deep and heavy. He wanted to have her that way, and every way, again and again. Baby or no baby.

And so without even thinking about it, he followed the haphazard urge to pick up the phone and dial her number.

"Hello?"

"Good morning, beautiful."

"Derek," she said. Did she sound as enraptured to hear his voice as he felt hearing hers? "Hi."

"Listen, honey—I know everything we talked about last night, and that we didn't come up with any good answers, and I'm not sure what to do about it. But the one thing I do know is that I want to see you."

Her voice was a soft lilt on the other end. "You do?"

And Derek told her another truth. "No, it's more than that. I *need* to see you. I don't know what'll happen between us, I don't know how to solve our problem, but…just say you'll see me tonight."

As he waited for her answer then, he felt strangely adolescent, like a twelve-year-old boy asking a girl to a middle school dance. And it wasn't the first time she'd made him feel that way. And as for that heart-bending thing—well, it happened so often now that it had almost started feeling normal to him. Hell, just like talking to cats and babies.

"Does tonight…include Emmy?" she asked.

And he hesitated. He'd known it would be that way, of course. He just hadn't decided how to deal with it. *This is what happens when you move full speed ahead without a plan.*

"Yes, tonight includes Emmy," he heard himself say then. Because what other answer was there? If he was seeing Holly, then he was seeing Emily, too. Something Aunt Marie had once told him came rushing back to him now. *If you're gonna jump in the fire, do it with both feet.*

"That makes me so happy," she said, her voice brimming with joy. "And I'm so glad you called. After last night...well, I was afraid we were...you know, just done."

Like before, he hesitated. And then settled on still more honesty. "Maybe I thought that, too," he confessed. "But I couldn't help myself. I woke up with you on my mind."

HOLLY AND DEREK had agreed to have dinner at a nice Italian restaurant—a little fancier than his normal haunts—nearby. He liked the idea of actually taking her on a real date—even if he was still a little bummed out about the fact that there would be a baby in tow. Still, it wasn't as if he *disliked* Emily. And when he weighed it, this was far better than the alternative—not getting to see Holly at all.

When she came to the door, she nearly took his breath away. She wore a simple, fitted black dress and a short strand of pearls around her neck. And though he loved her hair down, tonight it looked elegant and classy pulled loosely up off her neck.

"You look great," he said, wishing his voice hadn't come out sounding so breathy.

She smiled a bit bashfully. "So do you." He'd dressed up a little more than usual, too, breaking out a collared shirt and dark pants, and since he didn't have much occasion for such clothes, he was pleased she approved.

"Where's Emily?" he asked, looking around. He hadn't exactly meant to ruin what would probably be their only truly private moment of the night, but other than the evening of Holly's seduction, he couldn't remember having ever come into her house without seeing the baby right away.

"She's taking a late nap. I'll go get her and we can be on our way."

He slid his hands in his pockets as he stood waiting in the living room. *This is okay. Even if there's a third party on our date, it still feels good to be taking her someplace nice. And we can still have a great evening.* Baby or not, he looked forward to the coming hours.

"Em dressed up special for you, too," Holly called from the bedroom.

And he let out a small laugh in reply. "She did, did she?"

"Mmm-hmm," Holly said. "She insisted on wearing her best outfit tonight."

He looked up to see them both appear in the doorway. As promised, Emily was indeed decked out in a black dress adorned with tiny pink rosebuds, complete with a white lace collar. She wore ruffled white socks and tiny black patent leather shoes with buckles. She even had a little pink bow somehow attached to her minimal hair. He couldn't help smiling.

"Wow, Emily," he said. "And I thought your mommy was hot."

He looked up to find Holly casting an amused grin his way.

"Don't worry, Mommy," he said, placing his hand on her shoulder and leaning in to drop a quick kiss on her cheek, "I don't go for younger girls."

The sound of her laugh filled his senses. And then she handed the baby off to him, and together they got her buckled into her carrier and ready to go. Holly looped her purse and the diaper bag up over her arm, then reached for Emmy's carrier with the other hand.

"I can get it," Derek said, picking up the carrier. She had her hands full already, after all.

As the trio moved toward the front door, the phone rang—and Holly groaned.

"Can you let it go?" he suggested.

"No," she said on a sigh, "it could be about my mother. Emily and I dropped by the hospital for a while earlier and things were fine—and Michelle arrived as we were leaving, so I've assumed things were still going okay, but…"

Derek set Emily's carrier on the floor and knelt down

over her while Holly headed to the kitchen to answer the phone. The baby was smiling up at him and, somewhat to his surprise, he found himself smiling back.

"Got your belly," he said softly, reaching to tickle her tummy through the dress. He'd seen Holly tease the baby with those words and remembered her being quite entertained by it.

True to his memory, she giggled.

"Oh, you like that, do you?" he said. He tickled her once more, watching her tiny gold-flecked eyes light with joy.

But when he sensed Holly behind him, he quickly stood and turned to face her, promptly wiping what he suspected was a very silly smile off his face. "Ready?" he asked.

Only she released a long, heavy sigh and her distressed expression said it all. "You won't believe this."

Damn. Already he knew their night out was not destined to be. "What?"

"My mother has taken a slight turn for the worse. The doctors aren't worried, but Michelle still thinks we should both go to the hospital just in case."

"Then you should," he quickly told her.

"But what about our date?"

Despite his disappointment, he attempted a smile. "We'll get around to it," he said. "Don't worry."

"You must hate me," she replied glumly.

"No, I…" *I love you.* God, he'd almost said that. "Of course I don't hate you, silly," he told her, recovering.

But damn. *I love you?* He couldn't believe it.

Or hell—maybe he could. He'd pretty much felt it begin to happen back with that very first bending of his heart in her driveway on the day they'd met, and he guessed he'd just been barreling in this direction ever since. No matter how crazy it sounded to him.

"I'll stay here with Emily," he told her.

But still—love? *Love?* He hadn't expected that. And yet, here it was, in one sense wrapping around him warmer than anything he'd ever felt, and in another slapping him brutally in the face.

"Take as long as you need—we'll be fine."

So, this was it—the thing poets wrote about and singers crooned about and young girls cried over. Well, at least that explained how wonderful and how horrible he'd felt lately—at the exact same time.

"Oh Derek," Holly said, "I'm so sorry to do this to you. You don't *know* how sorry."

And it was the words she'd just said—along with the distress written all over her pretty face—that finally shook him from his big revelation. Because hell, on top of everything else, he didn't want her to be sorry. He wanted her to know it was okay and that he would help her through this however he could.

"Hey," he said softly, "I just went through this with Aunt Marie. I understand. You need to be with your mom."

She peered up at him with wide eyes. "How can I thank you?"

And despite all the uncommonly tender feelings pulsing through him, Derek felt a wicked grin sneak onto his face. "I'll be thinking of ideas while you're gone."

Her lips curved into a tiny smile, but it faded quickly. Looking completely depressed, she raised on her tiptoes to give him a kiss on the cheek—then she handed him the diaper bag. "There's a bottle and a jar of baby food in here."

"Drive carefully," he told her.

She nodded, sad expression still in place, and he watched her walk out the door.

He wasn't thrilled about the prospect of spending another night alone with Emily, but he really had no choice. Offering to sit with her had been the only decent thing to do. And besides, he truly *did* want to help ease Holly's troubles.

"Well, Em," he said, glancing down at the velvet-clad baby, "looks like it's me and you—all dressed up and no place to go."

"Ah gooo."

He bent over the carrier and unhooked the strap that held her in. Then he looked around the room at his choices of baby paraphernalia. "Swing?" he offered. "Bouncer thing? Quilt?"

"Gaaaaa," she said, looking up at him.

"Oh hell," he muttered—then he picked her up and walked to the couch. No reason he couldn't hold the kid.

He positioned her sideways in his lap and peered down at her. "I don't mind your company, Emily," he told her. "I really don't. But that doesn't change the big picture, you know."

Because despite how easy it might seem in certain moments, and even despite the obvious rewards—namely Holly, Derek knew he simply couldn't get involved in this child's life.

After all, he might screw it up. What did *he* know about being a parent?

Besides, maybe he didn't really want to care about someone in that all-consuming way.

Too late.

He wasn't sure where those words had come from, but if he was in love with Holly, well…so far, that pretty much showed every sign of being awfully damn consuming. Which made this whole situation even more of a problem.

"But I'm not even going to think about getting attached to *you* like that, Em," he told her. "Nothing personal. You're a great baby, but…I just can't. You understand. You need somebody who can…be a real daddy to you. A guy who knows what he's doing. I'm lucky just to be keeping you alive here, you know? You deserve somebody who…well, who was cut out for this. And I'm not. The fact is, I must have been last in line when they handed out dads, because I got a pretty lousy one. So I didn't…um…get the proper training."

He realized then that Emily was gazing up at him very intently, and so he quieted his ramblings and met her gaze head on. He looked deep into her eyes and tried to guess what was going on behind them, tried to understand what she felt, tried to imagine the kind of person she would be when she grew up. He thought about some of the difficulties she would face along the way to adulthood—probably just the usual: acne, peer pressure, waiting for the right boy to ask her to the prom.

Still, he imagined a father could come in handy during those hard times. And he knew better than most people that it was important for a child to have a dad. So thinking about Emily not having one suddenly pinched his heart.

"After all," he said, smiling softly down at her, "whose gonna scare your boyfriends into having you home on time?"

She smiled back at him. "Aaaaa."

"And whose gonna walk down the aisle with you at your wedding?"

Her eyes widened. "Aaaaaaaaa."

"And whose gonna tell you that there's no way you're wearing that dress out of this house, young lady?"

She giggled, then tilted her head, still peering up at him with great big eyes. "Gaaaa."

And he suddenly began to get the idea that...

"Oh-h-ho no," he told her, "don't look at *me*, Em." Frustration washed over him, with a dash of confusion added for good measure. "I mean, haven't you heard a word I've said?"

Then he sighed. "The fact is, Emily," he told her quietly, "I'm just not the right guy for the job."

Chapter Eleven

D EREK STRAPPED EMILY into her carrier seat, picked
it up, and then walked next door. Things had been
getting a little too heavy there for a minute, so he'd
decided to lighten the mood.

"Claws," he called, stepping inside. "Here, Claws."

"Meow," the white kitten answered instantly, frolick-
ing from the kitchen.

"Hey, pal," Derek said, stooping to pick up the little
cat.

He'd decided that maybe Emily and Claws would
like each other. And even if they didn't, he sort of
thought he'd been neglecting his new cat. Seemed kind
of mean to adopt a cat, then leave it at home alone all the
time. "Wanna come over to Holly's with me tonight?"

"Meow."

"Big party going on," he explained wryly. "Yeah—
me, you, and Emily. Didn't want you to miss it."

Then he returned to the other house, cat and baby in
tow.

Once inside, he extracted the baby from the carrier

and lowered her into her swing. He turned the swing on low, setting Emily in motion before he took a seat on the couch. Then he watched as Claws made himself at home, tentatively exploring some of Emily's floor-strewn toys with one outstretched paw before finally curling into a ball at Derek's feet.

Derek tried not to let himself think about Holly, or wonder when she might be home and if their evening might be salvageable. Neither of the other two times he'd sat with Emily had their evenings continued very favorably afterward.

Well, of course, after their talk last night they had kissed a little. But frankly, he was thinking about the sensual magic that had passed between them the evening before last, the one when Emily had been away.

So it seemed more sensible, and less frustrating, to think about... "Feeding," he decided aloud.

"Meow."

"Not you," he said, casting a chiding glance down at the kitten. "The baby."

"Aaaaaa," Emily replied.

"Right," he replied, "you." But first, he thought, pretty as Emily looked, he should probably change her into something more casual. He wasn't good enough with the baby spoon yet to risk her good dress.

He carried her to her room and lay her on the padded table where he'd changed her diaper on previous occasions. Using one hand to steady her, he reached with the other into a drawer on the chest next to the padded table. "Are you in a pink mood?" he asked, eyeing the pink cotton sleeper he held in his hand.

"Ahgoooo," she cooed at him.

Minutes later, he returned the more casually dressed Emily to her swing in the living room. "Ready for some dinner?" he asked.

"Gaaaaaa," she happily replied.

So he dug past diapers and stuffed toys in Emmy's bag until he located a bottle and a jar of strained sweet potatoes. "Mmm," he said, making a face to the contrary. "Orange mush. How delicious for you."

He uncapped the bottle and slid it into Emily's waiting mouth, balancing it until her tiny hands reached up to hold it.

"I'm thinking about livening things up tonight," he told Emmy as she drank. "What do you think?"

She didn't reply, too absorbed in her bottle. So he looked to Claws. "Music?"

"Meow."

He nodded, then rose and went to Holly's sound system, near her TV. A few seconds later, he found his favorite local rock station on the radio—but when the loud music came blasting out, he flinched and quickly reached for the volume knob, turning it down low. He didn't want to hurt Emily's ears.

"There," he said, looking to Claws. "See, I told you it was a party. Food, music—" he cast a glance at Emmy, "—girls. We have it all, Claws. We're a couple of wild men on the loose here."

Digging in the diaper bag once more, he came across a bib featuring Tigger. Then he settled on the carpet beside Emily, removed the lid from the jar of baby food, immersed the baby spoon inside, and pried Emmy's lips away from the bottle, setting it on the floor beside them.

"Waaaaa," she said softly.

"Don't get upset," he told her. "I just need to put your bib on you. See, it's Tigger," he said, holding it up. She smiled at the bib, which pleased him.

Tying it around her neck, he fed her a few bites of the so-called sweet potatoes, glad to see she liked them better than applesauce. Like before, he reinserted the bottle from time to time for the sake of variety.

An hour and a diaper change later, Derek felt it was safe to say the three of them were bored. He flipped off the music since it clashed hideously with the tinkling sounds that came from Emmy's various musical toys. "Party's over," he told Claws. "But you're obviously too drunk to drive. Why don't you stay here and sober up for awhile."

Derek got down on the floor with Emily, who lay on her quilt looking desperate for some kind of entertainment. But lullabies were definitely out.

On impulse, he reached one finger in between the snaps of her sleeper, tickling her tummy through her T-shirt. She giggled, and he smiled down on her with wide eyes. "What's that?" he asked in the most ridiculous voice he'd ever used in his life. "Is there a little snake in your sleeper?"

He reached in and used his index finger to tickle her once more and another laugh from her made his heart feel warm. "Say 'There's a snake in my sleeper, Claws, and it tickles'."

Derek wasn't sure how, but soon he had put his words to music and shaped it into a song. Still tickling with his finger, he sang. "There's a snake in my sleeper, there's a snake in my sleeper."

Okay, it wasn't much of a song. So he decided to add a twist—dropping a letter each time he sang it. "There's a nake in my leeper, there's a nake in my leeper. There's an ake in my eeper, there's an ake in my eeper."

After finishing his newly composed tune, which, to his pleasure, seemed to entertain Emily immensely, he scooped the baby into his arms and moved to the couch. Then he glanced up and unexpectedly caught sight of himself in a mirror down the hall. It was an odd picture. He cuddled a baby in his lap. And a small white cat lay perched near his shoulder.

"Look at me," he muttered. Yep, he'd lost his edge—that was for damn sure.

And yet he couldn't help but feel deep down inside as if he were...getting something else in return. He couldn't put his finger on it and wasn't really sure he even wanted to—but it was there, hovering around him like a thin mist, and it felt safe and it felt good and...

Okay, wait just a minute here—this is getting ridiculous. Spending so much time with a baby must be zapping my brain cells or something. Or maybe I'm just tired.

And so whatever it was he was feeling, he vowed to just not think about it anymore.

HOLLY STAYED VERY quiet as she peered in through the screen door. Although she'd had to cover her mouth and stifle her giggle during the "snake in my sleeper" song. And this man didn't think he was cut out for fatherhood? Holly suddenly didn't think she'd ever heard a more ludicrous statement in her life.

Look at him. Just look at him and Emmy. And even Claws, too. Derek might not think he was daddy material, but she'd never seen anyone who looked cuter or more content in the role.

After they'd settled on the couch, Holly finally came inside. "Hi," she said, toting a large shopping bag at her side.

"Hey, you're home." Derek looked up with a smile. "I didn't expect you for a while."

"False alarm," she explained. "Mom's back on track again, so she insisted that Michelle and I both leave. In fact, she even forbid us to come back tomorrow."

He nodded. "That's good news. I'm glad she's doing okay."

"And how are *you* doing?" she asked, casting a soft grin his way.

"Oh, me and Emmy and Claws, we're doing great. Aren't we, guys?" Neither cat nor baby responded in any way. "Well, we are," he told her.

She held up the shopping bag to ask, "Hungry?"

"Do I smell Italian?" he inquired hopefully.

"Antonio's has takeout," she informed him. "I wasn't sure what you liked, so I took a guess and got a double-order of lasagna."

"Perfect," he answered, his mouth curving into a warm smile.

Holly walked to the dining room table and began unloading her wares. "I also got...bread," she said, pulling out a long, narrow loaf, "wine—" she extracted a bottle, "—and candles." She drew those out last.

"Good timing," he said, "because I'm starving."

"It's the least I can do for you, considering all you've done for me," she told him.

"Although," he added with a glance down at the baby, "Emmy's looking kind of dressed-down for dinner now. I didn't want to ruin her dress, so I changed her."

"I'm glad you did," Holly replied. "And besides, Emmy won't be joining us for dinner tonight."

He lowered his chin. "She won't?"

"When Emily's Aunt Michelle found out that you and I had been cheated out of yet another date," she explained, "she offered to babysit for a few hours so that you and I can have some private time."

"Private time," Derek echoed. "That sounds...nice." His dark, sexy eyes pinned her in place and she was glad she could offer him this little interval without Emily. As much as she loved her daughter, there *were* times when it was good to be alone and she'd been looking forward to it for the entire drive home.

Holly walked to the living room and lifted the baby from Derek's arms. "Michelle's waiting outside in the car," she told him. "She'd keep Emily for the night, but she's got an early appointment in the morning. I'm going to swing by and pick her up in a few hours."

"'Night, Emmy," he said as Holly wrapped her in a light blanket and strapped her into her carrier. She'd already fallen asleep.

Just the thought of being alone with Holly had Derek's temperature rising—he couldn't wait. And while Holly took Emily outside, he set the table, grabbing plates from the kitchen and pulling two candleholders off a shelf in the dining room. Next, he rooted through a kitchen drawer until he found matches, then lit the candles. After dimming the lights, he pulled two stemmed glasses from the small china cabinet next to the dining room table, uncorked the wine, and poured.

When he was done, he cast a quick glance at Claws, who'd meandered into the room behind him. "Looks like maybe there's a party after all. Just a different kind now. And sorry, but you're probably not invited to this one." He dropped a quick wink to the cat—just as Holly came back in the front door.

"Oh my." She lifted a hand to her chest with a light gasp. "This looks lovely."

"All I did was set it out," he told her. "You were the one who brought it all home."

"Well," she said, as they both sat down, "I really

wanted us to have a nice evening."

"I have a feeling we will," he said, suddenly more hopeful than he'd thought possible considering the way the night had begun. He lifted his wineglass in a toast. "To you," he said. "The most exciting woman I've ever met."

He liked the way she blushed. "*Me? I'm* the most exciting woman you've ever known?"

He gave his head a sly tilt. "Have you forgotten the other night? Or, I mean," he joked, "was that just kind of run-of-the-mill for you?"

This time the color that rose to her cheeks was accompanied by pretty laughter. "You know it wasn't," she said, looking bashful. "You know it was unusually…"

"Mind-shattering?" he asked with a devilish smile.

She nodded as she sipped her wine. "Um, yeah," she said, "mind-shattering about sums it up."

Derek couldn't keep his eyes off her as they ate and chatted—about Holly's mother, about Emily, about Claws. He liked watching her lips move when she talked, drank, ate. He liked watching her every move—the tilt of her head, how her tapered fingers lifted a glass or a fork, the dainty way she blotted her mouth with a napkin. His heart had been doing that bending thing since she'd walked in the door, and the sensation grew stronger throughout the meal.

God, she was beautiful. And God, he loved her.

Damn, that was still a shock. But he was getting a little more used to the idea now, beginning to accept it.

He was beginning to get past the stark fear part to the this-feels-so-damn-amazing part. He was in love with Holly Blake.

When they'd finished eating, she rose and cleared the table while he poured two more glasses of wine. And by the time she rejoined him, he didn't think he could wait any longer. All his feelings seemed to have gathered in his pants, emotions and physical urges all melding into one huge ball of desire.

"You look beautiful in that dress," he told her across the table.

She answered warmly. "Thank you."

"Let me take it off you." The words came in a rough rasp.

Another pretty pink blush found her cheeks as she bit her lip and peered at him over her wineglass. "Are you in a hurry?" she asked playfully.

"Yes," he told her, deciding not to mince words. "We don't get much time alone so far—so when we do, I want to squeeze everything into it that we can. And ever since I left your bed the other day, honey, I've been waiting for the moment when I could have you again."

Holly's beautiful green gaze turned darker, sexier, than he'd ever seen it before, and it pinned him in place as she said, "Well then, consider me dessert."

Chapter Twelve

DEREK'S SWEET, DAINTY Holly had once again surprised him with how utterly hot and sensual she could be. And if the pressure in his pants had been powerful before, now it was officially overwhelming. He wanted her. And he wanted her now.

Rising from his seat, he walked around to her side of the table and pulled out her chair, allowing her to stand and face him.

"Turn around," he whispered.

She hesitated only for a moment, biting her lip. Then she did as he'd asked, facing the table again.

As he placed his hands on her shoulders from behind, even that slight, small touch set small fires deep inside him—he'd never known a woman who could arouse him so much, so easily. And part of him wanted to just stand there, to let his fingers rest on her delicate shoulders, to bask in that simple pleasure. Yet despite his wish to prolong the moment, he found himself reaching for the zipper at the back of her dress and smoothly sliding it to her waist.

Taking in the bra strap that crossed her pale back, he reached up to her shoulders again, this time gently pushing the dress down off them. "Take it off for me," he breathed low in her ear.

When she turned back toward him again, he took a few steps back from her so that he could see her, study her.

She lowered the dress to her waist, then pushed it gracefully to her ankles and stepped free of it until she stood before him, her luscious body clad in only a sexy black lace bra and matching panties.

"Unh…" He heard the soft moan escaped him.

"You like?" she asked.

"Very much," he murmured on a nod, studying the swell of cleavage that peeked from behind the tight lace.

He lifted his eyes to her face and watched her bite her lip. "I've had these for…well, a while," she explained, sounding suddenly timid. "But I've never worn them."

He tilted his head. "Why not?"

"I've never…felt comfortable enough, or sexy enough…like I feel when I'm with you."

Derek couldn't wait another second—he stepped up and took her in his arms, pressing her into a kiss. And when the hardness in his pants meshed with the softness between her legs, she released a sweet moan.

"You feel so good," he breathed as his palms skimmed over the lace, relishing every curve that hid underneath.

"Mmm…" she replied, and he kissed her mouth, her

cheeks, her eyes, her nose.

Then he ran his hands over her throat, her chest—her skin like velvet to his work-roughened fingers. Raining kisses on her neck, he slid one bra strap from her shoulder—then lowered his mouth to the porcelain skin there, following with still more delicate kisses across her silky flesh. Soon his fingers found their way to her lace-covered breast, stroking lightly at first, then taking it full into his hand.

"Kiss me there," she whispered.

"Mmmmm," he growled, excited by her candid yet somehow innocent command. And, eager to obey, he gently peeled the black lace down to free her breast, then lowered his mouth to its enticing pink peak.

"Oh—oh Derek," she breathed over him. He circled her taut nipple with a stiffened tongue, then lifted his hand to the lace of her other breast. "Ohhhh," she moaned.

As enraptured as he was with her beautiful breasts, though, he wanted more of her. He was almost surprised at his own impatience, but then he chalked it up to the one thing about Holly that was different than any the other women he'd known before: He was in love with her.

He lifted his kisses back to her neck as he slid one hand to the lace-covered spot between her thighs. "Ahhhh..." she nearly purred when he touched her there, and his chest tightened with increasing need.

Reaching around the thin swath of lace, his fingers

found the warm moisture they sought. "I want to kiss you…here," he said, sinking his touch further into her wetness.

"Oh God," she sighed between rapid, gentle intakes of breath.

Derek started to slowly strip the bits of lace from her body, caught off guard to discover his hands were trembling. But it didn't matter. Holly trembled along with him, each touch becoming as powerful as an electric jolt.

When she was naked, she reached up to unbutton his shirt—and he wrapped around her, pressing his bare chest against hers and cupping her bottom in both hands as he lowered a warm, thick kiss to her lips.

Lifting her onto the table, he pushed her legs apart. And he drew his attention from her only for the length of time it took to lean around her and swiftly blow out the candles. "Things are gonna get hot enough without these," he whispered. Then he drew her back into his embrace as he began to kiss his way down her body, lingering at her throat…her breasts…her stomach.

"Oh Derek," she breathed above him as he moved closer to where he'd promised to kiss her. "Derek, I've never…"

On his knees now, he licked her belly button—but her words made him stop to look up at her. Was it possible? No one had ever loved her this way before? "Is it all right?" he whispered.

She nodded vehemently. "Yes," she said between

still-rapid breaths. "I want you to do everything to me."

Using his hands to spread her thighs farther, Derek bestowed the first tiny kiss between her legs and listened as a moan escaped her throat above him. It fueled his fire and he used his tongue to slice deeply into her wetness, the muscles in her legs tensing sharply beneath his fingertips as she cried out in passion. His heartbeat reverberated throughout his whole body.

He listened to her labored breath above until his own desire reached peak intensity. He wanted to make her feel better than she ever had in her life. He worked at her sweetness, felt her moving against his mouth, her undulations coming harder and harder, until finally, finally…he heard her release.

"Ohhhh! Oh God! Ohhhhhhh…"

Even when her sounds softened, though, he continued bestowing soft kisses and licks there, aware of a selflessness he'd never quite experienced before. It filled him with satisfaction just to know he'd taken her there, given her that perfect piece of heaven for a few incredible seconds.

When he stood up, Holly leaned back over the table, her body looking long and slender, her hands planted behind her for support. She'd let her eyes fall shut.

"Good?" he asked her softly.

Her eyes fluttered open and she offered him a gorgeously wicked smile. "Mmm, good…" she breathed.

"I'm glad," he told her.

"Now…"

"Now what?"

"Now come inside me."

At this, another of her sweet commands, he undid his pants and quickly complied, pushing easily into her soft, waiting body. "Aw baby," he breathed, soon lost in the ecstasy of her.

As she raised herself against him, he pushed in deeper, as deeply as he could. And he moved against her, trying to go slow, but unable to still the heat that pumped through his veins.

When her arms closed around him, his body took over, pumping harder and harder into her. He couldn't remember a moment in his life when he had ever felt more consumed, or more connected to another person.

"Don't wait, Derek," she told him, her voice coming in feathery breaths. "Come for me."

"Oh…" he moaned. And though he'd actually wanted to stretch this out, take his time, she'd just pushed him over the edge.

He let go then, let it happen, let his body and mind dissolve into a million tiny points of heat and light that reached every extremity in his body. He closed his eyes and gripped tight to her hips as the thick pleasure burst through him.

HOLLY WATCHED HIM sleeping. He was beautiful.

Then she glanced at the clock by her bed. One a.m. And tomorrow was Sunday. Ah—what could be better than sleeping next to the man she loved and knowing that the next day was entirely theirs, with no alarm clocks to rule the day?

"Uh waaaaa." Though the soft sound rising from the other room almost shocked her somehow—Emily was home now. After their hot sex on the dining room table, she and Derek had gotten dressed and driven to Michelle's house to pick her up. And really, it had all worked out very well. Holly wanted to be alone with Derek, but she also wanted to have Emmy near her, too. Maybe she *could* mesh these two worlds, after all.

Pushing back the covers, she got up and reached for her robe, tossing it on and tying it loosely in front.

"Waaaaaa."

Then she rushed into Emily's room and quickly lifted the baby from her bed.

She settled with her in the rocking chair in the corner, where a streetlamp shone through the window, providing enough light for them to see each other. "Did you have a bad dream, punkin?" she asked the baby, who had quieted at her arrival. "Did my sweetheart have a bad dream?"

She rocked in the chair with Emmy in hopes of lulling her back to sleep.

And she thought about the things she'd done with Derek tonight.

Soon maybe she'd be bold enough to let herself do those things without sending Emily away—to feel that freedom, that sense of rightness about it. Derek had a way of taking away her inhibitions, of empowering her, giving her the courage to face her desires head on and stop running from them.

She remembered experiencing such passion as a teenager. But she supposed she'd squelched it—nice girls didn't feel those things. Finally now she realized: She *was* nice, and she *did* feel those things. And how horrible to have found it necessary to swallow such beautiful, alive emotions. It had taken her this long to get them back. It had taken *Derek* to get them back.

Why did I ever push those feelings down in the first place? She wasn't sure. Maybe her parents' divorce had confused her about sex, or maybe her father's departure from her life had confused her about men.

But whatever the reason, now she let a smile form on her face in the darkness. How wonderful to discover that her fears had been in vain, that she *could* do the things she wanted and follow her urges, that she *could* be so wild and reckless.

"Well, time to put you back to bed," she whispered to the baby in her lap who neared sleep once more. "Time for me to get back to Da—"

Oh. Oh God. She'd almost called him *Daddy.*

Her heart sank instantly at the realization. Because yes, in one sense, things were wonderful—completely perfect. But in another, it felt like an empty victory if Derek wasn't willing to share *everything* in her life, Emmy included. And she wasn't sure where he stood on that *now*, but only twenty-four hours ago he'd informed he didn't *want* to be anyone's daddy.

And yet maybe…

Maybe if she eased Derek into Emily's world at the same time she eased *herself* into the dual roles of mother and lover…

Maybe all of them would discover how wonderful it could all be.

Though…it was probably wrong of her to hope so fervently that Derek could change his mind about being a father. After all, he'd made his position perfectly clear.

And still, she couldn't stop hearing him singing the "snake in my sleeper" song to Emily earlier. It rung in her ears, and in her heart.

Looking down, Holly realized that her daughter had fallen back asleep. So she rose slowly from the rocker and gently lowered the baby back into bed. "Sweet dreams," she whispered.

Then she padded quietly back into the bedroom, slipped off her robe, climbed back beneath the covers naked, and cuddled up against the man she loved. She thought she could get used to this. If only…

DEREK LAY ON top of Holly, nuzzling her neck, raining soft kisses beneath her hair. "You're beautiful," he whispered.

She kissed his lips in reply.

And he couldn't help smiling at the woman next to him in the darkness. Despite his earlier fears, this had turned into another wonderful and very heated night with her. Even now, the sleeping, the holding—all of it felt so damn good.

Next to him, she yawned.

"Tired?" he whispered.

"Mmm-hmm," she said. "The last few days have been…"

"Busy," he finished for her, chuckling.

"Besides this," she said, motioning to the bed, "there's been my mother's heart attack, and of course…you've learned all there is to know about babysitting."

The last part had come out sounding hesitant and he understood why. They hadn't talked any more about the problem that still hung over their relationship. And he didn't particularly want to. He was having too good a time to let anything spoil it.

"Derek," she began, again sounding tentative and filling him with dread, "do you mind…sitting with Emmy…very much?"

He sighed, still not wanting to go into this now. "No," he said anyway. "I don't mind helping you out when you need a favor."

"But what I mean is…"

"Holly," he said quietly, "I think I know what you mean. And I don't think this is a good time to talk about it."

When she stayed quiet, he felt like he'd yelled at her even though he'd only whispered the words. So in way of apology, he reached out and found her hand beneath the covers, gently squeezing.

"Derek," she said softly, "the thing is…"

He sighed and he closed his eyes, not wanting to have this conversation. It was the middle of the night and he was half asleep. Who knew if his explanations would make any sense? And most of all, he didn't want to hurt Holly's feelings. If they were going to discuss this, couldn't they wait until he was awake, when he could think straight?

"The thing is," she continued, "that this feels like…something serious to me, what you and I have."

"It *is* something serious," he confirmed.

"Then—"

Damn it—she wouldn't stop. "But what I feel for you doesn't change the way I feel about having a family."

There, he'd said it. It was out now. And it was a horrible thing to tell her after their sex earlier, but she'd just kept forcing the issue.

Still, when she didn't reply, he felt guilty. And he knew that—like it or not—he had to say more, try to explain. "Holly," he began, "I love you, but—"

"You love me?"

He hesitated. *Aw hell—this is what I get for talking about important things when I'm tired.* But there was no point in denying it now. "Yeah," he admitted quietly. "I love you."

He heard her quick intake of breath next to him. "Oh Derek," she said. "I love you, too."

He sighed as her words washed over him, sank in, and then seared his heart. Because…he hadn't expected this. Just because she'd seemed crazy about him…well, he'd still just assumed that he was the only one of them who would leap so fast to calling this love. And to hear that he wasn't, that she felt it too, made him feel a little dizzy, even lying in bed. "Really?" he asked.

"Yeah, really."

She loved him, too. Damn—he hadn't even dared to ponder the possibility. It was amazing. And horrible. Because she was the woman of his dreams—the sweet woman with a sexy side who he hadn't even known he wanted. But the fact that she loved him…well, it also made everything just that much more complicated. Unrequited love might be easier than this.

"Holly," he pressed on, "the thing is, even though I love you…"

"Yes?"

"I'm…just not sure, honey."

Even in the dark, he could sense her eyes clouding over, could feel a heavy new weight settling over the room. "About what?" she asked.

And he let out a sigh, just wishing she would let this go for now. But she wouldn't. And so as much as he hated to hurt her, he had to be honest. "About us. About the future."

"Because of Emily," she said.

Derek couldn't help feeling ashamed. But he said, "Yes," anyway. It was the truth.

Even in the shadows, he caught sight of something glistening on her face—a tear rolling down her cheek. And he wanted to reach for her, hold her, love her. But he was afraid to right now, afraid that reaching out would be equivalent to conceding, to changing his mind.

But would that really be so bad?

The question burst through him like a ray of sunshine, but before he could form an answer, old memories clouded his thoughts and took hold of his judgment.

Every single moment you spend with a child molds them, shapes them, adds to their perception of the world. Every wrong move counts. Every stupid word spouted in anger, every grimace or frown—all of it goes straight to a child's heart.

Derek knew all that was true—he'd found out the hard way. And now, the very idea of being put in that same position, of trying to mold a life, trying to always make the right decision…it was too overwhelming for him to even think about.

He couldn't bear that kind of responsibility—he simply couldn't, and wouldn't.

HOLLY OPENED HER eyes and shifted her gaze to the clock. Four a.m. Then she rolled over on her pillow and looked at Derek. She studied his eyelids, his nose, his mouth. She listened to him breathing and noticed the lock of hair that had fallen over his forehead.

She thought back to earlier when he'd told her he

loved her. He'd just said it—like it was nothing big, nothing shocking, like something he was totally comfortable with. And it had filled her with joy…but only for a painfully-too-short moment.

If only he could be as comfortable with the idea of fatherhood. And even though she knew that was making quite a leap—going from *I love you* to being a daddy—in her heart, the chasm didn't feel quite so wide. She'd seen him with Emily, after all.

He'd looked nervous that first night when she'd invited him to cook out, but that had changed as the days had passed. Now he looked completely at ease taking care of her. And whether he knew it or not, he also looked completely content. In her heart, Holly was convinced more than ever that Derek would be the perfect father for Emily, no matter what he thought.

"You'd be perfect," she heard herself mumble sleepily.

"Hmm?" She watched his eyes ease open, saw his gaze shining on her in the darkened room.

"Nothing," she murmured, still half asleep. "I just said you'd be perfect."

"Perfect for what?" he mumbled back.

"A perfect father for Emily."

She saw him shaking his head against the pillow. "Nope," he muttered. "Too much responsibility, too hard to be a good parent, don't know what I'm doing."

"No one goes into it prepared, Derek," she explained, waking up more fully. "It's a learn-as-you-go experience, and you just do the best you can."

He reached out and pulled her to him, gentle but firm, in the dark. "Let's not do this, honey," he whispered near her ear. "Let's just sleep. Let's just rest and hold each other."

Holly sighed and settled against him—what other choice did she have but to do as he asked? And being in his arms—sleeping with him, holding him—was like heaven. The only hard part was trying to ignore the shadow of doom that seemed to hang over their love.

Chapter Thirteen

———— ✤ ————

FIRST HOLLY HEARD Emily crying in the next room. "Waaaaaaaaa! Waaaaaa! Waaaaaaaa!"

Then she heard Derek moan beside her. "Geez…"

She sighed. Who was she to push him into fatherhood if he didn't want it? He had been right about one thing—you had to really want it if you were going to do a good job of it. She suddenly felt stupid for her murmurings in the night. She should have just left well enough alone.

"Waaaaaaaaa!"

"What's wrong with her?" Derek asked.

Holly finally opened her eyes as daylight streamed through the curtains, alerting her that it was morning. "She's hungry."

"Waaaaaaaaa!"

"I'm gonna go get her," she said, starting to push back the covers.

But to her surprise, Derek reached out and grabbed her wrist.

"What?" she asked.

"Didn't you get up in the night already?" He sounded as weary as she felt.

"Twice," she told him. "She had a fussy night."

"Go back to sleep then."

"Derek, I can't. She's hungry."

"I'll get her," he said.

And Holly couldn't believe his words. "You'll what?"

"I'll get her," he told her, this time sounding a little impatient, almost as if he was annoyed at having to repeat himself. "What do I need to do?"

"Well, make a bottle, but—"

"How do I do that?"

"The stuff's on the kitchen counter. You just mix powder and water. The instructions are on the can, but—"

"Okay then," he told her. "Go back to sleep."

Still dumbfounded, she watched as he reached for his underwear and pants, then lumbered from the bedroom. She lay there utterly stunned and confused. What on earth was happening here? She didn't feel completely assured that he was awake and alert enough to read the instructions on the powdered formula correctly, but that was actually secondary to her bigger concern.

Let me get this straight. He doesn't want to be a daddy to Emily, but he wants to get up and feed her when she cries first thing in the morning?

That made no sense whatsoever. But she didn't let that stop her from getting out of bed, throwing on her robe, then sneaking furtively to the dining room where she could peek around the corner to the kitchen unnoticed.

"Don't cry, Emmy," he was telling the irritable baby who sat in the carrier on the kitchen floor. "I'm mixing it, I'm mixing it."

She watched him hold up the can and paraphrase the directions aloud. "One scoop of this stuff for every two ounces of water." Then he shifted his attention to the counter, to the clear bottle with the pale pink teddy bears dancing around the sides. "And this is…an eight ounce bottle. Four scoops."

"Meow." Claws trotted past Holly and into the kitchen, where he rubbed up against Derek's ankles.

"Hey buddy," Derek said, sounding less than energetic. "You're just in time to feed the baby."

"Meow."

"Oh," he said, looking down at the kitten, "I get it. I guess you're hungry, too. Well, give me a minute—the baby comes first, and then I'll get you some milk."

"Meow."

"Then, next time, *you* can make *me* breakfast and feed the baby. Sound like a good deal?"

"Meow."

"Hold your horses, Emmy, it's coming," he said, shaking the bottle vigorously. "Here we go," he said, finally lowering the yellow nipple to her mouth.

Holly listened as silence consumed the house. Then she realized Derek was watching Emily eat. He stayed kneeled before her, his eyes full of tired affection, his mouth half open, appearing almost mesmerized with her motions. A lump formed in Holly's throat.

"Meow," Claws said impatiently, breaking the silence.

"Sorry," Derek said, turning to face the cat. "I forgot." He then rummaged through Holly's cabinets until he found a small dish and turned hurriedly to the refrigerator. He soon lowered a bowl of milk to the floor for an anxious Claws, who wasted no time lapping it up.

"There, everybody's happy now," Derek said, standing up to survey the situation—and then he gave his head a short shake. "Geez, you guys are a handful." But Holly didn't think he sounded like he really minded.

Quietly, she crept back to the bedroom. Derek had gotten up specifically so she could sleep, after all, so she didn't want him to think she hadn't taken advantage of his generosity.

And besides, she *was* pretty tired—the last few days had truly been exhausting, in some ways that were bad and in some that were definitely good. She closed her eyes, choosing to remember the good parts—like last night on the dining room table.

Then she sank quickly into sleep, comforted that Derek was with Emily. All seemed right with the world.

SHE AWOKE TO a scintillating kiss.

"Mmmmm," she breathed, letting her arms wrap around his neck.

"Morning, beautiful."

"Good morning," she whispered, opening her eyes to his warm, inviting gaze.

"Sleep good?"

She nodded. "Thank you for getting up with Em this morning. That was sweet."

"Well, I love you," he told her by way of explanation.

"I love you, too," she said, lifting her mouth for another kiss.

"So, listen," he said, "remember when you invited me to the zoo? For yesterday? You didn't go without me, did you?"

She pulled back slightly, pressing her head more deeply into the pillow, a little taken aback by the weird question. "No. In fact, with my mother being in the hospital, I forgot all about it. Why?"

"Well," he said, "I was thinking—why don't we go today?"

Holly just lay there, feeling a little numb. Was she hearing things? This made no sense. First he gets up to feed Emmy at dawn and now this? "But I thought...you didn't..." Her voice trailed off helplessly.

"Thought I didn't what?" he said as if he had no idea what she could possibly be talking about. "I'd like to go with you and Emily to the zoo. Okay?"

"And, um, just what brought on this sudden urge to visit the zoo, Mr. Cassidy?" she asked pointedly, arching one brow in his direction.

Just then Claws pounced onto the bed, walking up

between them on the comforter.

And, reaching out to pet the cat, Derek innocently replied, "Well, I obviously like animals."

DEREK TOOK HIS change from the cashier, then worked to balance the soft drinks and a box of popcorn in his hands. Turning from the concession stand, he spotted Holly, and Emily in her stroller, waiting across the concrete walkway that wove a path through the zoo. Holly looked beautiful in a pair of white shorts and a summery top that revealed a soft shadow of cleavage. Emily wore a sleeveless dress with a sailboat appliquéd on the front.

"Help," he said, reaching Holly. "I'm about to lose the popcorn."

Holly came quickly to his rescue, saving the popcorn and relieving him of one of the cups.

"Where to next?" he asked.

"I believe the bears are just around that bend," she said, pointing ahead of them.

"On to the bears then," he replied—and he instinctively reached out to begin pushing the stroller at the same time as Holly.

"Oh," she said, clearly taken aback at his silent offer. "You...don't have to."

"Well, you have your hands full," he pointed out matter-of-factly. "You man the popcorn, I'll man the stroller."

"You're not gonna get much popcorn that way," she said laughingly as they proceeded down the path.

"Maybe you can feed it to me," he said playfully, then opened his mouth.

She reached for a couple of the fluffy white pieces, but then stopped, sounding very serious when she said, "I can't."

"Why not?"

"I just saw a sign that said 'Do not feed the animals'."

As she glanced up at him with gorgeous green eyes, he couldn't help laughing. Though for some reason, the joke brought to less-amusing thought to mind. "I wasn't much of an animal last night, though," he said quietly. "I mean, compared to four times the first night, one seems like…almost nothing."

She smiled. "Don't worry—you still rate animal status. I judge on quality, not quantity."

Carrying his soft drink in one hand, and pushing Emmy's stroller with the other, he leaned down for a quick kiss from the woman who so brought out the animal in him. "Mmmmm," he said, letting his lips linger near hers. Then he murmured, "You're kind of making me feel like an animal right now."

"Oh, look," she said suddenly, pointing. "Polar bears."

And he glanced ahead and caught sight of an enormous white bear in the distance.

He stopped the stroller—but a crowd gathered

around the large, rocky pit where the bears were located and he knew Emily couldn't see them. So he reached inside the stroller and lifted her out, using both hands to hoist her up over his head.

"Look, Em," Holly said, peering up at her daughter. "Look at the big bears."

A few minutes later Derek lowered the baby gently back into the stroller, tickling her stomach and offering a soft bear growl that made her smile.

And when he extracted his head and straightened his body, he found Holly smiling at him, her eyes alight.

He glanced away, though. He loved the woman, but he didn't want her getting any funny ideas. Just because he had invited them to the zoo, and just because he wanted Emily to be able to see the bears, didn't mean anything.

Not that she could really perceive what she was seeing anyway, he realized, but it had still somehow seemed important that she get to see them.

He gave his head a brisk shake then, trying to clear various bits of confusion away.

The truth was, he really didn't know how he'd ended up in this position.

Feeding the baby early this morning had been one thing. He'd thought about how hard Holly worked and how she probably never got any rest and then how she'd been under extra stress because of her mother's health. He'd fed the baby for Holly.

But the zoo? He wasn't sure what had made him ask

her to go, what had come over him. The sun had been shining in the kitchen window with the promise of a gorgeous day and Emmy had been cooing up at him in between drinks of her breakfast, and...well, it had just seemed like a great day to do something outdoors. So when he'd been lying in bed with Holly an hour later and the thought occurred to him, he'd acted on impulse.

Now, here he was, walking with Holly, pushing a stroller, even thinking about buying Emily a balloon or something, and he had to admit—hell, he was having fun. His feelings about Emily had certainly changed since the moment he'd first met her, which seemed like months ago instead of just a few short days.

To his further surprise, he even found himself thinking that he might not be enjoying the zoo quite so much if he were here with Holly alone. Yeah, he knew Emily was really too young to really see the animals or to understand why they'd brought her there, but...maybe seeing the animals with Emily was helping Derek to see them, too. In a way that maybe he never really had before.

Oh, sure, he'd been to the zoo. But never with his father. Being here with Emily was helping him to see it through a child's eyes.

In fact, he felt almost as if he were seeing it through *lots* of children's eyes. They were all around him, with their families, taking in all the sights and sounds and smells of the place. And it occurred to him now that anyone who saw him with Holly and Emily would assume that they, too, were a family.

But that doesn't change anything. He needed to stay grounded in reality, after all. And he wasn't any more cut out for fatherhood today than he had been yesterday.

"Look! Gorillas!" Holly said, breaking into his thoughts. And glancing up, he saw that another crowd surrounded this habitat, too. He automatically reached in the stroller and lifted Emily to see.

HOLLY PULLED IN the driveway, anxious to get home, both to Emily and to Derek. Despite her mother's wishes, she'd wanted to stop by the hospital today, so after they'd returned home from the zoo, she'd left the baby with Derek. Her mother had been moved out of intensive care and into a regular room, and if all continued to go well, she would be home in a few days.

On the drive back to the house, she'd stopped and picked up some steaks to cook on the grill. And she bounced merrily up on the front porch and was about to step inside when something brought her to a standstill. Was that Emily she heard giggling? The light, airy sound wafted out through the screen door, making her smile.

She didn't exactly want to spy on Derek, but...she couldn't help herself. She snuck up to the door and peeked in, unnoticed.

Emmy lay on the floor on her quilt and he sat beside her. He'd removed her little canvas tennis shoes and gently shook one tiny blue-sock-covered foot in the air to the beat as he sung the old dance song, "Shake Your Bootie".

When she accidentally rustled the bag she carried, he immediately went quiet and shifted his eyes toward the door. Uh-oh, the jig was up.

She stepped inside and found his uneasy gaze resting on her.

"Sorry," she said with a soft smile. "I didn't mean to sneak up on you guys."

"You, uh, weren't really supposed to see that," he told her sheepishly.

And though she didn't want to embarrass him, she figured it was time to come clean. "Well," she admitted, "I'm afraid that's not *all* I've seen."

At which he raised his eyebrows in silent inquiry.

"I know Emmy has a snake in her sleeper, too," Holly told him, watching his face color.

"Wow, is nothing sacred?" he finally said. "Can't a man spend time alone with his…his…girlfriend's baby without being spied on?"

Holly smiled. *Is that all Emily is? Your girlfriend's baby?* The words were dying to come out, but she didn't want to push it, so she held them inside. Watching him feed Emmy this morning had touched her deeply. And the trip to the zoo today had been wonderful. So maybe all of that was enough for now. Whether or not he wanted to admit it, Holly knew he was starting to care about her daughter. So instead she just said, "You really are a great guy, you know that?"

"Look," he said, still sounding sheepish, "so I sing to the kid. No big deal. Really."

And again, Holly wanted to say so many things. She wanted to tell him that yes, it *was* a big deal. She wanted to tell him how she loved nothing more than watching him with Emily, and how she suspected that Emmy was starting to become very fond of him, too.

But of course she still couldn't say any of that without fearing his denial of it all, so this time she simply kissed him, pressed her lips warmly to his, felt his mouth ease open beneath hers, inviting her tongue inside—and she let her body fill with more of the incredible passion only Derek had been able to release in her.

When the kiss finally ended, both of them were breathless.

And he said, "Maybe I should let you watch me sing to the baby more often."

DEREK SPENT SUNDAY night at Holly's house, too. What they shared in the darkness was slower, sweeter, than their previous sex, and she sensed a new tenderness in the way he touched her, in the way he moved inside her.

After, as she lay with her head on his broad chest, she whispered to him. "That wasn't quite...the usual fare."

He misunderstood her comment. "Was it...kind of boring?"

"No," she replied, shaking her head vehemently as she lifted it from his chest to peer into his eyes. "It was…kinda nice."

"Oh," he said, a soft smile stealing over him.

When the alarm went off the next morning, she felt like some kind of dream weekend had ended. Monday felt so different from Saturday or Sunday—the work week was upon them and her hectic schedule of daycare and school and daycare again had returned. Even as she lamented the end of the lovely weekend they'd shared, she found herself pushing back the covers and rushing to begin her day. There was so much to do in an hour's time.

After her shower, she woke Derek, who seemed surprised to see her standing over him, already dressed for work. She suspected the sensation of losing something in the end of the weekend had struck him, too.

"I'm sorry if I seem in a hurry," she said, rushing around the room, rummaging in her jewelry box, looking for shoes in the closet. "But I'm running a little late and I haven't even dressed Emmy yet."

He nodded from his spot in bed, but stayed silent.

"You can have the shower if you like, though," she said hopefully. After all, he had to work, too—her life wasn't the only one with a schedule, even if hers was more rigid.

Twenty minutes later she met up with him in the living room. He'd just emerged from the bedroom, showered and dressed, as she was dashing to Emily's room to pack the diaper bag. She only wished she understood the strange, silent tension that she felt growing between them.

Although, deep inside, she feared that she *did* understand it. She feared that it was the same tension that had been present all along—they might have managed to push it aside for a while, but it hadn't vacated the premises.

Still, she hoped against hope that she was wrong, that she was imagining it. She was rushed and he was sleepy, that was all. It didn't mean things were changing.

"Derek," she said when they met up and stopped, face to face, in the hallway. She knew she sounded—oddly—surprised to see him amid her own personal morning rush hour. But she didn't know what to say. Things suddenly felt too weird.

"I'm gonna get going," he told her. His voice sounded the same, and he looked the same. But somehow something *was* different.

And she had to take a chance, see where she stood. So she did the only thing she could think of—she assumed their relationship would continue on the same track that it had these past few days. "So," she suggested tentatively, "dinner?"

And Derek answered only by glancing briefly into her eyes, then taking her hand and leading her to the couch.

Dread gathered into a tight ball in the pit of her stomach as they sat down together, as she waited for the ax to fall. No, she wasn't imagining the tension at all—it was thick and heavy and lay over the room like a smothering blanket.

And then he lifted his fingers and gently touched her cheek. "I love you, baby, but…"

Her heart hurt. She'd known it was too good to last, yet she supposed the past couple of days had given her a false hope she'd wanted to believe in. And she considered making it easy on him, finishing the sentence for him, yet why should she? "But what?"

"But we're moving so damn fast here…" he told her softly.

"And?"

"And I'm not sure I can make it to the finish line."

Holly sighed, and then—unable to fight down an instinct that leaned toward desperation—tried to be cheerful, tried to make him see things another way. "Then don't think about the finish line. Just think about the race. We race well together, don't you think?"

"We race together perfectly," he told her. "But I'm…"

Holly took a deep breath. "Scared?" she offered. She knew it was a strange attribute to apply to a strong, virile man like Derek, but…

"Maybe," he told her softly. "At any rate, I just think it might be smarter, for all our sakes, to…slow things down a little."

"I see." She didn't mean to sound so cold, but she knew it had come out that way.

Because it felt like rejection—maybe not of her, but of her daughter. And hell, maybe of her, too. Moving too fast. That kind of spread the rejection around in her mind—it was a rejection of…a little bit of everything.

And what it boiled down to was that he still just didn't feel the way she wanted him to. And she supposed that wasn't his fault, but it wasn't hers, either.

And it hurt. Dreams for her, and for her daughter—new ones she'd built just over the last couple of days, but which felt as real and vibrant and palpable as if they'd already come into being—were crumbling almost as quickly as they'd been unwittingly formed.

"Holly," he said, lifting her chin with his fingertips, "this doesn't mean I don't love you. It doesn't mean I don't want to be with you. I do. And it isn't that I don't…care for Emily. But…" He swallowed visibly and Holly knew he was stuck on what else to say, how to explain his feelings. One thing she could say for Derek—he'd never led her on and she knew he never would. He wasn't the kind of man to make promises he couldn't keep.

"It's all right, Derek," she told him. "I understand."

"Do you?" he asked. "Because—"

"I do," she promised him. She understood all too well. And she needed to end this conversation before she fell apart. "I need to go now," she said. "I'm late dropping Emily at daycare and you probably need to get ready for work yourself."

"Yeah," he said, sounding sad and halfhearted—and she was glad. She hoped he *was* sad. She began to feel angry with him because she could almost see the truth in his heart and she knew he was simply too afraid to follow it. He loved her, and he wanted to love Emmy, too—but he was a coward.

Too afraid to love a little girl. Damn him.

He slowly rose to go, but Holly stayed on the couch. She knew she would start to cry soon, and she desperately wanted him to leave first.

"Bye," he said quietly, nearing the door.

That was when she spotted Claws sitting across the room on a bookshelf, looking like one more knick-knack. "You forgot your cat," she told him.

"Oh…" He walked across the room and scooped Claws up with one hand—then the two of them left.

As soon as the door shut, she let her tears leak free. *Some father* he'd *make. He can't even remember to take care of his cat, let alone a baby.*

So it was just as well. Emily didn't need a man who didn't want her. And Holly didn't need that man, either.

Then why are you sitting here crying like a little girl?

Apparently Derek Cassidy had successfully unlocked more kinds of girlish emotions than just passion. And despite herself, she still wanted him more desperately and wildly than she'd ever wanted anything in her life.

Chapter Fourteen

———∼————

HOLLY SAT AT the faculty table in the cafeteria, absently shuffling the tater tots on her tray. It was only lunchtime and the day had already been a long one.

She tried to tell herself it was no different than any other day. After all, before last week, she hadn't even known Derek. He'd been nothing more than her new neighbor, the guy with the loud music blaring from his truck. She'd had no idea he was someone she could fall in love with.

Fortunately, though, she went through the motions easily enough. After all, she was used to hiding her feelings at school. She never let on to missing Emmy as much as she really did—it would be unfair to her students. But today she missed more than just Emmy. She missed Derek, too. Even though he would still be next door to her tonight, she felt as if he'd suddenly moved much farther away.

"Holly, are you all right?"

She looked up to find the principal, Mrs. Harrington, a stout woman in her fifties with tidy hair and impeccable taste in suits. She tried to smile. "Oh, I'm fine, Mrs. Harrington," she said. "Thanks for asking."

The woman reached down to pat Holly's hand, then moved on. The entire staff, of course, knew about Bill's death and they never pressed her for answers when she seemed a little down. How surprised they'd be to know that today's depression had absolutely nothing to do with Bill whatsoever. Today's emotions were caused by someone new in her life, someone totally unexpected. And yet, it felt like he'd been in her life, in *their* lives, forever.

Three hours later, she stood outside watching the students run for the big yellow buses that lined the school parking lot. She thought of Emmy, of the fact that one day, probably before Holly knew it, her daughter would be one of those children, out in the world, facing school, friends, recess, bus rides, and everything else that came with growing up in this life. And it saddened her to think that Emmy would do all that without a father. Having had her own father leave when she was ten, Holly's fondest hope for Emily had been a solid family to depend upon. But…no father at all was better than one who didn't love her.

When Holly and Emily returned home that afternoon, Holly was quick to rush inside. Derek's truck wasn't home yet, but she didn't want to bump into him. In fact, she suddenly wanted to stay as far away from him as possible. She'd gotten the message this morning, after all. And as the day had worn on, the more it had hurt and angered her.

"We don't need him," she told Emmy as she unhooked the car seat and lifted the baby into her arms. They'd done just fine by themselves before he'd come along, and they'd *continue* doing fine. They were both better off without him.

DEREK SENT HIS men home at the regular time, but he decided to stay on the job site a little late. After all, there was nothing to go home to, he thought as he hammered a nail into a two-by-four. Well, there was Claws, but frankly, he was a poor substitute for the strawberry blonde next door.

He'd spent the whole day wondering just exactly what had happened between them this morning. One minute they'd been snuggled in each other's arms and the next, he'd started *feeling* weird, she'd started *acting* weird, and everything had fallen apart.

Grabbing another nail from the pouch at his hip, he tried to refocus on work.

He couldn't make sense of it, but it had been like waking from a great dream only to be delivered to the blandness of reality. Maybe he'd felt a little abandoned to roll over in bed and find Holly gone. Maybe returning to the real world of work and alarm clocks and other commitments had disillusioned him. Things had suddenly seemed surreal enough that he'd felt the need to get back into his own surroundings. Like it might be better to slow down, safer to put some distance between his life and Holly's. Like maybe he had some thinking to do.

"Damn it," he muttered, smashing his thumb with the hammer. How long had he been doing this kind of work, and still he couldn't manage not to hurt himself? So much for refocusing on it. *This was all her fault. He'd spent all damn day being distracted by her.*

"Aw hell," he grumbled, "may as well go home." If he was going to be plagued by thoughts of Holly, he could do it just as well there. And possibly without inflicting injury upon himself.

When he pulled his truck into his driveway a little while later, he quickly perused the surroundings. Holly's car was home, but he saw no sign of her or Emily outside. Which was best.

He hadn't expected her to react so coldly to his refusal this morning. And was it even that, a *refusal?* No, not really. She'd blown everything out of proportion. He understood that she had to be protective of her and Emmy's interests, but just because he didn't want to have dinner didn't mean he was calling things off. Why did women have to make everything so dramatic?

Turning the key in the lock, he stepped in the front door to see certain kitten come trotting around the corner to greet him. "Hey, Claws," he said easily. "At least I know where I stand with you, pal."

He reached down and scooped the white cat up into his hand and used the other to stroke his furry little throat. He guessed he'd gotten pretty attached to old

Claws in a short time.

Of course, the same could be said for Holly, and even Emily. But that was different.

After all, Claws was a pretty self-sufficient guy. He didn't require that much care.

He lowered the cat to the floor, but the little furball proceeded to climb up his leg, hooking his claws into Derek's old blue jeans. "You're a little clingy, a little needy," he told the cat in retrospect. "And you definitely live up to your name. But other than that, you're okay to have around."

Derek changed clothes, fed the cat, made himself a sandwich, and checked the mail. Life seemed normal for the first time in a week.

Normal…and a little dull.

"What did I do for fun before Holly and Emily?" he asked Claws, who had shadowed his every movement since he'd come home.

"Meow."

Oh sure, he did things. He met his friends at baseball games or got together with them to shoot a few hoops. He sometimes stopped in at the neighborhood bar near his old apartment to drink a beer with the regulars. He dated girls who were often pretty and showy and whom he seldom cared anything about. And more recently, he'd spent time dealing with Aunt Marie's estate, then doing work around the house after moving back in. But the work was mostly done now and the estate was settled. And as for those previous activities, something about them suddenly sounded meaningless.

Meaningless? Since when had he become such a deep guy that everything he did required meaning?

Well, maybe the last several days had changed some of his perceptions about things. Or…maybe he was just losing his mind.

He shook his head, remembering when life had felt simpler. Before Aunt Marie had died. Before his pretty neighbor had seduced him. Before he'd learned how to change a diaper and stop a baby from crying.

Being with a baby had been a new experience for him—hell, a whole new world. And it hadn't been as bad as he might have expected. But it didn't change the facts. He was the last guy in the universe who was ready to be a parent.

And yet, nonetheless, he'd spent the whole damn day thinking about the two females next door. "This is getting ridiculous," he muttered.

As boredom gripped him, he almost felt a little stupid. He'd refused dinner tonight as if he had something else important to do, and now he half-regretted it. He and Claws would both be having a better time if they were over at Holly's house with her and Emily.

"But I'm not about to call her," he told the cat. After all, a guy had to stick to his guns and that was exactly what he planned on doing. "Now hop on up here." He patted the couch cushion next to him, then turned on the TV. "Playoffs are starting and it's time for you to learn about baseball, young man."

THE NEXT DAY, Derek gave in and picked up the phone. Dropping a gaze in Claws direction, he said, "So much for sticking to my guns, right?" But he couldn't help himself. He was lonely. And except for Claws and his work, life suddenly felt strangely empty.

Not that he was going to tell her that. He would just play it cool. He'd never had a problem doing that with women before Holly and Emily had come along. He only hoped he could pull it off now.

"Hello," she answered.

Damn, her voice was pretty. *But get your game face on.* "Holly, it's Derek."

She hesitated, and when she replied she suddenly sounded removed, distant. "Hi."

He decided to ignore her tone, suggesting, "I thought we might get together tonight."

And this time her hesitation was shorter. "No."

"No?" he asked, taken aback. "Just plain 'no'? Not 'no, I'm really tired', or 'no, I have other plans'? Just 'no'?" He knew he was no longer acting cool, but hell, why pretend?

He heard her sigh loud and clear over the phone. "Okay, how about—no, I've finally realized that this was a bad idea from the beginning and that I was stupid to get involved with you in the first place. Or perhaps—no, because I have a daughter, as well as a very hectic schedule, which makes me unavailable for wooing every second of the day, and it's clear that's not conducive to your lifestyle. Would either of those answers satisfy you more?"

He sat there for a minute, dumbfounded, before he found his voice. "So that's it?" he asked then, irritated and not even trying to hide it. "I don't respond exactly the way you want all the time, so it's not even worth trying to work things out?"

"Derek, there's nothing to work out."

She'd said it so easily. It sounded so final. And it made his blood boil and broke his heart at the same time. "I see," he said. "Fine, then." And he disconnected the phone.

"Meow," Claws said, staring intently up at him from below.

"Quit lecturing me," he told the cat. Then he stalked from the room.

He plopped on the couch and turned on the TV. Flipping through the channels, he found another baseball game. But after a couple of strikeouts, he quickly realized that he really didn't care about baseball at the moment.

So he turned the TV back off, trudged to the kitchen, and pulled a can of beer from the fridge, popping the top. Maybe he would just get drunk. Maybe it would take his mind off her.

"What did I do so wrong here?" he asked Claws, who again tailed him everywhere he walked in the house. He'd asked the woman out—he'd even taken her and Emily to the zoo. He hadn't realized he was making a lifetime commitment.

Lowering himself back down on the couch, he lifted Claws into his lap, willing himself to feel calmer. After all, if she wanted to play it this way, he should probably be happy. He didn't need her *or* Emily. He and Claws we're better off like they were—"Just a couple of bachelors in our bachelor pad," he said.

And yet...hell. Despite himself, he couldn't help looking around Aunt Marie's house and thinking how much she'd have liked Holly if she'd gotten to know her. He wished his aunt were here to ask for advice. He'd learned to value her opinion over the years and now he missed it. She'd always seemed to know what was right for him—from the time he was a troubled teenager right up until her death.

His mouth twisted into a bittersweet smile when he remembered that Aunt Marie had been harping on him to "find a nice girl and settle down, for heaven's sake," just a few days before she died. He wondered how she would advise him now, knowing—as she had—how he felt about children and parenthood.

He had a feeling he knew the answer. And suddenly he didn't want to think about the things she might tell him. In fact, suddenly he could hear her voice curving around words and phrases she had used at other times in his life—"follow your heart", "believe in your instincts", "have faith in your own feelings".

He sighed and took a sip of his beer, absently stroking Claws' back while the kitten purred. What it all came down to in the end, he supposed, was that he missed Holly. And maybe he even missed Emily, too.

But that didn't mean he wanted to be her father. Did it?

Or did it even matter now that Holly seemed to regret ever laying eyes on him?

BY FRIDAY AFTERNOON, Holly knew it was stupid and pointless to continue trying to avoid Derek. Not that she wanted to see him. Because she knew if she saw him it would only make her heart hurt. But she and Emily had lives to lead and they couldn't hide in the house forever.

Besides, what difference did it really make if she saw him? Her heart already seemed to hurt all the time anyway. There had been moments when she'd regretted being so rude and abrupt when he'd called the other night, but she still stood by her decision. She couldn't waste her time on a man who couldn't love Emily, too. No matter how crazy she was about him.

Holly stood at the living room window, Emily tooling around behind her in her walker. The lawn looked horrible—she was going to have to mow. And she thought the car was already out of wiper fluid after only a couple of drizzly days this week that had required using it, even though a certain someone had filled it not very long ago. Which meant maybe she had a leak. Great.

"Enh," Emmy said as she batted her little hand at a plastic ring that hung suspended on the front of the walker.

Holly sighed. She wished she could leave Emily in here while she did the outdoor chores—Emmy was getting so active with her play—but she just didn't have that luxury. So she'd have to interrupt Emmy's fun and set up the playpen outside, where she could keep an eye on her while she worked.

Glancing down at Em, their eyes met, which somehow added to Holly's guilt. Her daughter was reaching a stage where she hated being confined to the playpen. So Holly quickly decided to compromise.

It was a lovely early fall evening, after all—really too nice to waste completely on work—so she'd just put Emmy in her stroller, go outside and take care of the wiper fluid, and then they'd take a nice walk through the neighborhood. *Then*, if she had time, she'd mow. She knew, of course, that she probably *wouldn't* have time to mow, but she couldn't help wanting to cater to her daughter and enjoy life a little. She'd get to the yard work soon—just not tonight. She had the whole weekend to deal with it.

Holly put Emily in her stroller, then grabbed Eeyore and a rattle, hoping they might keep the baby entertained while Holly put windshield wiper fluid in the car.

Wheeling the baby into the yard near the driveway, she set the foot brake on the stroller, then opened the garage door. Inside, she found the half-empty jug of windshield wiper fluid perched on a shelf. And she tried not to think about Derek or the day they'd met as she pulled down the container and stepped back outside, then proceeded to lift the hood.

She glanced toward Emmy and said, "How're you doing, punkin?"

"Gaaaa," Emily replied, sounding quite content.

After which she turned back toward the car and her jug of wiper fluid. *Now, where did Derek show me to put this stuff?* Darn it, she couldn't recall. The car's inner workings looked just as puzzling as she remember.

"Let's see," she said, studying the blackened maze. "Seems like he said that the thingamajig was mounted on the…"

She stomped her foot in frustration—why couldn't she remember something so simple?

Well, maybe because your entire life has been turned upside down since that day.

In fact, it was odd, but Holly thought that adjusting to life without Derek, even after the short time they'd known each other, was somehow actually proving more difficult than adjusting to life without Bill had been.

DEREK SAW HER from his porch. Damn it, she still looked just as gorgeous as ever.

And the scene felt too damn familiar—he didn't want to remember that this was how it had all begun between them. In fact, he wanted to turn around and march right back inside.

But—he sighed—he still couldn't resist a lady in distress, even if that lady had made it very clear that she didn't want or need him around.

And though he knew it was a dangerous move, he approached her anyway.

"What's the problem?"

Holly withdrew her gaze from the car to glare at him. "I can't find the damn windshield wiper fluid container thing," she snapped.

His eyebrows narrowed. "I just filled that for you, not two weeks ago," he pointed out. "It shouldn't be empty already."

"I didn't think so, either," she admitted. "I've used some of it, but not that much. And I'm already out."

"Must have a leak," he said, taking the fluid and easily pouring it in the car. "I can pick up a new receptacle and put it in for you."

"No thanks," she said in a biting tone, crossing her arms as if to emphasize the words.

He looked at her in surprise—more than a little taken aback by her complete indignation. He'd known she probably wouldn't act overly nice—but *this* was how she wanted things to be between them? "'No thanks'?" he asked. "Can't a guy even do a favor for his neighbor these days?"

Holly turned on him then, fuming, and he knew immediately that he'd said the wrong thing. "Oh, so that's all I am to you now, a neighbor?"

Derek sighed and raised his arms in despair. "I thought that was all you *wanted* to be."

"The way I see it, that's all you *choose* for me to be."

Oh brother—was she serious? He couldn't believe this! "You're kidding. I can't believe you're twisting this that way."

"Well, you made it clear that you didn't want to be with us."

"No, I didn't," he pointed out. "Just because I wasn't ready to make a lifelong commitment after a week, you threw me out of your life. I love you, Holly, but the trouble with you is that you demand all or nothing—there's no in-between allowed."

Holly took a deep breath. The words *I love you* rang in her ears, both warming and crushing her. And the rest of his words? She let out a sigh, absorbing them and…hell, really hating the fact that they almost made sense to her when she thought it through. She really *hadn't* given him too many options. But…it had felt like more than just a week.

Unfortunately, though, before she could figure out what how she wanted to respond to him, emotion got the best of her. It had been such a difficult period for her and before she knew it, it all came spilling out.

"Derek, I never expected to be alone, raising a baby. But taking care of Emily, working every day and having to bring work home a lot of nights, worrying about my mother—it's a lot. And you've been *so* wonderful about taking care of Emmy for me, and you added a whole new, fun, exciting passion to my life when I really needed it. But when you sulked around last Monday morning, I guess I just let it add to my stress and get the best of me. You're right—that it was only a week. But when you say you love someone, doesn't that sort of…go beyond time? Doesn't that make it a bigger thing? You say you love me, which is a wonderful feeling—but at the same time, I'm not sure you want to be leaned on—I'm not sure you want to deal with the hard times and not just the fun ones. I'm sorry there *are* hard times and not just fun ones, but that's where I am in life—and I'm not sure what to do with a man I love and want to be with, but who isn't okay with the whole package."

Derek stayed silent, and looked thoughtful, and Holly wondered what he was thinking. She hadn't exactly meant to blurt all that out, but it was the truth. Sometimes she needed someone to lean on. And for a few days she'd thought that someone might be Derek. But then all the tenderness she'd felt growing inside him had seemed to evaporate.

When awkwardness filled the air, she slammed the hood of the car and turn to Emily. Eeyore lay in the thick grass where Emmy had propelled him, so Holly stooped to get him and placed him back inside the stroller with her.

"Hey there, Emmy," Derek said softly. "Did you come outside to watch Mommy work on the car?"

But instead of letting herself be touched by the sweet warmth in his voice, Holly heard herself snap at him. "She's not like a cat, Derek. I can't just leave her in the house to fend for herself half the time."

Derek shook his head in clear annoyance. "For your information, Claws is perfectly pleased with the level of care and companionship I provide him."

And she got the distinct feeling that he'd missed her point. "Like I said," she steamed, "Emily is not a cat. It takes a little more to take care of a baby. It's a full-time commitment. The kind that sends guys like you running in the opposite direction."

"Hey," he said sharply, "I didn't decide to have a baby. I had no choice in this. And for your information, I happen to care about Emmy. I happen to care about her very much. So sue me if I was a little scared, if I wanted some time to adjust to the idea, to think about it. I…"

When his voice suddenly trailed off, Holly followed his eyes toward the lawn—where Mr. Nutter's German shepherd from across the street barreled in their direction in hot pursuit of a scampering squirrel—and bounding straight toward Emily's stroller.

Everything in that moment traveled faster than the speed of light, yet somehow in slow motion, too. Holly wanted to move, but her feet felt grounded in place. She hadn't strapped Emmy in yet—she had to get to her! Fear froze her body statue-still as the large dog sideswiped the stroller and sent it tumbling, tossing Emily free.

Chapter Fifteen

DEREK LUNGED TOWARD the baby, snatching her from the air and pulling her to his chest, then managing to twist his body to land on his back in the row of small bushes that lined Holly's front porch. He'd caught her with the skill of an NFL receiver snagging the winning touchdown.

The baby was screaming her head off, but all Derek could think was—*she's safe. Emmy's safe.*

"It's okay, sweetheart," he cooed to her, both of them nestled in the bushes. "It's okay, honey. I've got you."

When he finally lifted his eyes from the baby, he realized Holly was crying, too, both hands pressed to her chest. "Is she all right?" she sobbed.

"She's fine," he assured her, handing Emily up from where he lay. "She's better than me, that's for sure." The bushes had scratched his shoulders and back through his T-shirt and the stinging pain was starting set in.

"Oh my God, Derek," Holly said as she clutched the baby tightly to her, "are you okay?"

"Just some scratches," he said, finally freeing himself

of the gangly shrubs. "No big deal."

"Are you sure?" she asked, her eyes as warm as honey on him.

He nodded, finally getting to his feet and looking down on Emily to make sure what he'd said was true—that she was completely all right.

"Thank you," Holly said, her voice still wrought with emotion. "Thank you so much!"

But he could barely process her words. His heart pounded a mile a minute and he suddenly realized that Emmy's safety had taken the place of everything else in that horrible moment, and that he would have done anything to save her. He didn't know what he would have done, how he could have gone on, if he hadn't been able to catch her and keep her from harm.

Beside him, Holly began to rant and rave, cutting into his thoughts. "How could I not have strapped her in? How could I have been so negligent?"

But he placed one hand on her shoulder, using the other to rub Emmy's back as she snuggled against her mommy. "Holly," he began, "don't beat yourself up over it."

"But Derek, she could have—"

"Yeah, but she wasn't. Honey, no one can be perfect all the time."

"But I'd never have forgiven myself if—"

"You told me yourself," he pointed out, "that parenthood is a learn-as-you-go thing. You work so hard to be a good mother, but it's impossible not to make a mistake every now and then."

And it was then that he realized his own words almost startled him. Because they were pretty much the same she'd imparted on him not so long ago.

But he couldn't think about that right now—Holly was upset and he needed to comfort her. And hell, maybe he needed a little comfort himself—he was still pretty shaken up.

"You...wanna come in?" she asked, still teary-eyed. "I need to take care of Emmy, but...I could put something on your scratches, too."

Derek took a deep breath. She'd invited him in. And it wasn't the first time for that, of course. Yet he somehow had the feeling that if he accepted, everything would change. It was like standing on the edge of a precipice. Everything inside him was telling him to just close his eyes and jump. But at the same time, a strange, futile fear invaded him—a fear he couldn't fight down.

Holly watched his face, his eyes. It was as if some kind of panic had grown inside them—like she'd watched it take shape, forming visibly before her.

"Thanks," he said, sounding rushed, "but, um, no."

"No?" she asked softly.

"I'm gonna...go home and...call that idiot across the street and give him a piece of my mind, tell him to keep his stupid dog tied up."

Then she watched him turn and go, quick as that.

She knew he was running away, from the situation, from his fear, from her, from Emily.

Still, even now, that was all he could seem to do—run.

And she broke into tears all over again, not just from what had just happened, but also because she knew now that Derek loved Emily—she'd seen it in his eyes and heard it in his voice—yet he'd made it clear that he would never stop running away from them.

Once inside, Holly lay Emily on the couch and took off her sunsuit to examine her for cuts or scrapes. Amazingly, and thankfully, she found no evidence of the accident. The she put Emily's outfit back on her and sat on the couch, just hugging her. She thought she might sit there and hug her for the rest of the night.

But as she sat embracing her daughter, her thoughts returned to Derek. To the way he'd saved her child.

She herself had frozen in fright, but Derek had lunged to keep Emmy from crashing to the ground. It had all happened so fast, and yet he'd been there for Emmy—he'd responded by instinct. A *father's* instinct.

This just went to prove what Holly had feared all along, that sometimes a mother wasn't enough. Like she'd told Derek, and as he had just repeated to her, no one could be perfect all the time. And if Derek hadn't been there…well, she couldn't bear to even contemplate that. All she could think was—sometimes it took two people, two loving parents. That way if one of them messed up, the other was there.

It was all so clear to her now that it simply broke her heart. Derek loved her. And he loved her daughter. And they should be a family, damn it—a real family! They should be together, raising Emmy, and loving each other.

But somehow he couldn't see that. Or he chose not to.

What she'd had with Bill had been…nice. Pleasant, even. But what she felt for Derek transcended any emotions she'd known before. And it was all there just waiting for them, just waiting for them to reach out and grab it. If only…

She released a heavy sigh. *If only* had not gotten her very far with Derek. She should know that by now. No matter what happened, no matter what kind of love she saw in his eyes for her or her baby, it didn't change what he wanted, or what he *didn't* want, out of life. She was going to have to come to grips with that once and for all. But it was just so hard to kiss that dream goodbye. "Oh Derek," she sighed.

"Da," Emily said from her lap.

And Holly peered down at her. "*Da?*" she repeated, her eyes widening. "Did you just say *Da?*"

Holly fought the tears forming in her eyes as another heartbreaking sigh escaped her. "Oh Em, I think he should be your daddy, too," she told her little girl. "But *he* doesn't. And I can't have a man who doesn't want to be your father just because I love him. And apparently, it doesn't matter how much *either* of us love him, or even how much he might love us. It just isn't going to work out."

Holly sat battling a sense of loss and confusion, reminding herself that as much as the heart wants what the heart wants, the heart *didn't* want what it *didn't* want just as much. And that maybe it didn't matter why Derek didn't want to accept his feelings for her daughter—she simply had to respect it and move on.

After all, he'd done nothing wrong. And if he couldn't be *in* this the way she wanted from him, maybe he was doing them a favor by not pretending.

She was startled from her thoughts when the doorbell rang—and she looked up to find Derek standing on the other side of the screen door.

When he saw that she was still crying a little, he let himself in. And he'd brought Claws, who he lowered to the floor. He felt nervous. He didn't know why.

But wait—yes he did.

He had come back. And he'd come back for a reason.

"I called Mr. Nutter and let him have it," he told her quietly. But that wasn't the reason.

She nodded and he moved farther into the room, taking a seat next to her and Emily on the couch.

"Are you all right?" he asked. He didn't like seeing her cry, especially if he was the cause of it.

She nodded again and said, "Just…you know…still a little upset."

"Is Emmy okay?" Without planning, he reached instinctively to take her from Holly's arms into his lap.

Holly sniffed and wiped her eyes. "Yes, she's okay." Then she reached up and touched his arm. "But you're not," she said. "You're all scratched up."

He shrugged—the scratches were no big deal. "I've weathered worse," he said. "Claws, for instance."

"Meow," Claws said, leaping up next to them on the couch.

"I thought it might cheer Emmy up to see him," Derek offered, thinking how silly it sounded, but how natural it had seemed, for some reason, to bring the cat over.

Holly smiled at him through her tear-reddened eyes and it warmed his heart. It was the first time he'd seen her smile in a while and it reassured him. And gave him courage. The courage he needed more in this moment than ever before.

"You doing okay, Emmy?" he asked, shifting his gaze to look into the baby's eyes. And then he discovered that he'd missed those, too. A lot.

"I've been doing some thinking, Emmy," he said. He glanced up at Holly, but then lowered his eyes back to Emily and took a deep breath. He had made a decision. He wasn't gonna run anymore. And he was gonna quit fighting what he really wanted. He'd thought about Holly's words out in the driveway before and he'd realized—he *wanted* to be leaned on. By them both. "I've been thinking…that me and you and your mom and Claws would make a pretty nice family."

He heard Holly's gasp next to him, but he went on, his eyes locked on the little girl's. "I was thinking of asking your mommy to marry me," he said, "but she's been pretty mad at me lately, so I'm not sure she'd believe my heart's in the right place. I'm not sure she'd believe me if I told her how much I've missed you both and how much it scared me to see you in danger. So what I'm thinking is—I just try to talk her into believing in me, into giving me a chance to prove I can be the man she needs me to be. We give it a little time so I can show her—and you, too—that I'm in this for the hard times, too. What do you think?"

"Daaaaaa," Emily replied.

"Huh?"

"DaaaaDaaaa," she said.

Derek couldn't believe his ears. Or the warmth in his chest. He looked at Holly, amazed. "Did she say what I think she just said?"

Holly bit her lip and nodded. "Yes."

Then they both looked back at the baby in Derek's lap. He still couldn't fathom it.

"DaDa," Emily said again.

And suddenly, it all felt so right, so obvious. There were no more questions and no more fears. He was Emily's DaDa, and she needed him, and he needed her. Not to mention that her mother was the woman he'd been waiting for all his life. Aunt Marie's imagined advice had been true. He'd found the courage to follow his heart and trust his feelings and the world suddenly seemed perfect. *If you're gonna jump into the fire, do it with both feet.*

He turned to Holly, desperate to make sure he wasn't the only one feeling this way. "What do *you* think?" he asked her. "About me and you, and Emily, and Claws?"

Tears had filled her eyes again and she tried to sniff them back. "I think we'd make a wonderful family," she said. "But…Derek, are you sure?"

"Holly," he began, sighing, "my life's been empty without you. I want you and Emily. I want you to be able to lean on me. And I want to be able to lean on you, too. I want us to take care of each other, and to take care of Emmy, together. And like I said, I know I need to prove it—I need to show you. So that's all I'm asking— that you let me show you this is what I really want."

She sniffed again as her tears dissipated to be replaced with a beautiful smile. He returned the grin, and then he looked back to Emily. "And honey, I want you to be able to spend all the time with Emily that you want—so once I do show you, once you know you can be sure of me, you won't need to work anymore if you don't want to."

Her eyes went wide as she lifted her hand to her chest. Had she heard him correctly? "I…I won't?"

"I make plenty of money and nothing would make me happier than being able to provide for you and Em."

"Really, Derek?" she asked, her heart filling with a whole new kind of joy.

"Really," he replied with a smile.

Holly's chest flooded with a deep warmth. It seemed too good to be true. But it *was* true. She could stay home with Emmy, watch her every move, see her every smile, just as she'd always longed to. And then at the end of the day, the man she loved would come home to them both and their world would be beyond perfect!

"I love you, Derek," Holly breathed. Then she leaned over and nuzzled against him, content in knowing that she and Emily had found the man they were supposed to be with for the rest of their lives.

"Meow," Claws said, easing his way in between them.

And the right cat, too.

Look for more classic Toni Blake reissues, including:

The Cinderella Scheme

The Bewitching Hour

And don't miss any of these contemporary romance titles
from Toni Blake:

The Coral Cove Series:
All I Want Is You
Love Me If You Dare
Take Me All The Way

The Destiny Series:
One Reckless Summer
Sugar Creek
Whisper Falls
Holly Lane
Willow Springs
Half Moon Hill

Other Titles:
Wildest Dreams
The Red Diary
Letters to a Secret Lover
Tempt Me Tonight
Swept Away

About the Author

Toni Blake's love of writing began when she won an essay contest in the fifth grade. Soon after, she penned her first novel, nineteen notebook pages long. Since then, Toni has become a RITA™-nominated author of more than twenty contemporary romance novels, her books have received the National Readers Choice Award and Bookseller's Best Award, and her work has been excerpted in *Cosmo*. Toni lives in the Midwest and enjoys traveling, crafts, and spending time outdoors. Learn more about Toni and her books at www.toniblake.com, or sign up for her newsletter and follow her on Facebook to get all the latest news and have a chance to win signed books and other prizes.

Made in the USA
Lexington, KY
11 May 2017